I0739617

ISBN: 978-0-9945886-0-9

First published in Australia in 2013 by Kylie Chan
More information: www.kyliechan.com




Typeset in 10pt Sabon Lt Standard
Cover Design by Madeleine Chan
Printed and Distributed by Lightning Source (Ingram)

# The Gravity Engine

Kylie Chan

Michael waited quietly on the bench in the gardens of the medical facility. The garden was paved with red stones, and raised planter boxes held fragrant flowering shrubs. He looked at his watch; nearly time. He picked up the paperback next to him and pretended to read it, surreptitiously checking the path every thirty seconds. It was a few minutes before he realised he was holding the book upside down and he quickly righted it.

He checked his watch again; she was late. Michael stayed very still and tried to avoid fidgeting as he pretended to read the book.

He heard them talking before he saw them and sagged with relief. Clarissa's carer was pushing the wheelchair and Clarissa was a small, curled-up shape lost in the chair holding her. She stopped talking as they came into view and didn't meet his gaze. He turned back to the book, wishing that he could watch her with his Inner Eye, but she was an ordinary human and his Inner Eye could easily kill her.

He peeked at her over the top of the book and disappointment flooded through him again. Since she'd had the kidney transplant he'd hoped she'd regain some of her old strength, but she appeared as fragile and transparent as she always had: a shrunken, delicate, spun-glass figurine, twisted and deformed from the torture she'd suffered. Her hands were still rigid claws and her eyes were sunken and hollow, with the wide, unfocussed stare of those who'd been truly broken by the horrors they'd experienced.

For a moment he saw her face against the light, and he was thrown back to a vision of the woman he'd known and loved: strong, clever, vibrant and full of life. She'd suffered no idiocy from him and been a formidable partner and challenging lover. She'd been his whole world, full of courage and intensity, and had reacted with pragmatic curiosity when she'd found out about his father, the Tiger God of the West, and the complex nature of his Celestial family ties. Instead of being frightened she was curious and intrigued, asking him to show her his abilities and revelling in the feeling of going flying with him. She'd loved being engaged to a 'superhero' and had adored his tiger form. He promised to always protect her from the demon menace, and she trusted him completely.

The demons had taken her and performed vile experiments on her to create a clone that had completely fooled him for weeks – until it exploded. The Dark Lord of the Northern Heavens told him that the original was probably dead, breaking Michael's heart. Then the Dark Lord had infiltrated a demon nest and been shocked to find the real Clarissa a prisoner in the labs, patiently waiting for Michael find and rescue her. She came back a ravaged husk, nearly blind and unable to walk. Everything that had happened to her had been because she'd known Michael and he hadn't protected her at all.

The carer wheeled Clarissa out of sight through the garden and he leaned back on the bench and wiped his eyes, the novel forgotten.

Clarissa's psychologist appeared out of nowhere and sat next to him. 'What do you see when you look at her?'

'I see the good times we had together before all this happened. And a million regrets that I believed the Dark Lord when he said she was dead. I would have tried to find her – it never occurred to me that someone as powerful as him could ever be wrong.'

'You're still blaming the Dark Lord?'

'No, of course not.' Michael leaned forward, his elbows on his knees. 'I blame the Demon King. And myself, for not protecting her enough. He had her and my mother both —' His voice cracked. 'Both of them. My mother is dead and Clarissa is broken. The Demon King has a massive debt to me and I will ensure that it is paid.'

'And what about Clarissa?'

Michael studied his hands. 'I'm willing to wait for her as long as it takes.' He looked up at where she'd been. 'It tears my heart out to see her like this, but at least I can see her, and that's enough for me right now.'

The psychologist was silent for a moment, then said, 'She wants you to stop stalking her.'

'Okay, I'll stop,' Michael said.

'She knows when you're sitting there invisible. She knew when you did it before.'

'How?'

'She can smell you.'

Michael was horrified. 'What?' He sniffed himself; no serious BO – what the hell?

'You wear too much of that aromatic deodorant you young men tend to favour. It's all over you.' The psychologist leaned back and put her arms on the back of the bench. 'Despite the advertising, it's not attractive at all. Most women find it unpleasantly cheap and strong.'

'Then it's appropriate for me,' Michael said with a wry grin.

'No, it isn't. You may be strong, but your value is limitless. Youngest Worthy ever granted Immortality. Number One Son of the Emperor of the West. Running the West, and barely thirty years old. It won't be long before there's statues of you in the temples on the Earthly Plane, young man.'

'I wonder how they'll depict my half-European features.'

'Probably as unflatteringly as they depict your father's tiger ones.'

'Yeah.' He looked up at where Clarissa had been. 'I'll stop coming. But can you pass on a message for me?'

'She already knows that you'll wait for as long as it takes.'

'Any idea when she'll improve to a state where she'll actually be able to talk to me? I miss her so much …'

'You miss her and you want something with her. What if what *you* want isn't the best for *her*?'

'Tell me and I'll stay away for good. Say the words and I'll be gone.'

'What if she needs someone to support her without having any sort of relationship otherwise? Just to care for her?'

Michael lit up with a ray of hope. 'She'd let me look after her?'

'No sexual relationship, no kissing, no love, just to care for her. Could you do that?'

Michael couldn't believe what he was hearing, just being with her would be a dream come true. He didn't need the rest. 'I could do that? She'd let me?'

The psychologist studied him for a long time, then said, 'Stop coming here and throw yourself into your work for fifteen days. In two weeks and one day, come back here and do this again. I can't guarantee anything, but it may be different.'

Michael straightened. 'She might talk to me?'

'Give her two weeks of not seeing you here when she goes past, and her attitude when you return may be different.' The psychologist raised her hand when she saw his face. 'I'm really not promising you anything. When she sees you, she may ask for you to go away again. But having you here waiting for her every day at the same time has not just been an annoying distraction for her, it's been reassuring as well. Let's see how she feels when that reassurance is gone.'

Michael looked away and nodded. 'All right.' He turned back to the psychologist. 'Thank you. You've given me hope.'

'I hope I haven't done you a disservice; there's a good chance when you're back she'll tell you to go away again.'

'Should I stay away altogether? Would that be the best for her? All you have to do is say the words —'

'No,' the psychologist said firmly. 'I like to think that one day she'll heal enough to lead something approaching a normal life, and that includes a healthy relationship with you. The fact that you're prepared to wait means that you are the best one for her. So go away for fifteen days, and I'll be watching when you return.'

'Doctor.' He saluted her Western-style and disappeared to, as she said, throw himself into his work. There was plenty waiting for him.


'Hello?'

'Michael.' Enzio's voice was warm and generous. 'So good to talk to you. Finally! I've been trying for ages.'

'Oh,' Michael said. 'Sorry. I saw the messages, it's just been ...'

'No, I understand, my boy.' Enzio became even more jovial. 'So are you enjoying your new position? They're obviously keeping you very busy —'

*One, I need you in my office right now*, Michael's father said telepathically.

*On my way, my Lord.*

Enzio was still talking. '— And if you ever want to come back to us in Hong Kong —'

Michael cut him off. 'It's in my father's firm, Enzio. My dad's been very good about helping me, Clarissa was in a severe car accident shortly after both of us left —'

*NOW, One.*

*My Lord.*

'Oh that's terrible. Is she all right?'

Enzio's voice was full of sympathy but his falseness was clearly audible: Clarissa had been a second-quality staff member to him. He'd promoted Michael quickly even though Clarissa was obviously more skilled.

'She'll get there, but I have to go, my dad's in my ear, he wants me right now. Thanks for calling, Enzio —'

*ONE!*

'Bye.' Michael dropped his head and teleported to his father's office, then slipped his phone into the pocket of his White Horseman's uniform. The White Tiger, Celestial Emperor of the Western Heavens, was in human form; a muscular Chinese warrior with golden skin and white hair, sitting at his desk with a pile of papers in front of him.

'When I say now I mean *now*, One.' He waved for Michael to sit across the desk from him.

'Sorry,' Michael said. 'My old boss keeps harassing me about returning to work for him ...'

'This is a human, right? On the Earthly Plane?'

'My Lord.'

The Tiger shuffled the papers. 'And you're wasting your time,' he glared at Michael, 'being *polite* to this bastard? Block him. You have more important things to do. If I find you talking to humans again, I'll cut your fucking head off. Now.' He pushed the papers across the desk to Michael. 'Deal with this.' He rose and headed towards the door.

'Wait, this is the budget for the next twelve months — I helped Rohan prepare this! We need you to make a decision about whether —'

The Tiger cut him off again. 'No, you don't. You

make the decisions. I don't want to worry about it. I'll be in the harem, and if you disturb me, I'll cut more than your head off. Handle it.' He walked out.

*Rohan?*

*Yeah, Mike?*

*You were right. We have to make all the decisions. Meet in my office.*

*'Kay.* Rohan's voice filled with amusement. *Good luck making these calls – get it wrong and Dad will tear your head off.*

*I could resign and stand aside so that you're acting Number One Son until he finds a replacement …*

Rohan's mental voice became fierce. *Don't you fucking dare. See you in five.*

Michael had the budget open in front of him when Rohan came in and sat.

'You don't need me,' Rohan said. 'You're the most experienced one in the Western Palace for handling this sort of shit. Just do it.'

'I wish I had the up-to-date figures on the commodity markets, turning it into platinum, or something like titanium, might be more worthwhile,' Michael said. 'When I was back with Enzio, it was all in front of me. Who would I talk to about arranging it?'

'No,' Rohan said, 'delegate it. You have too much other stuff to worry about.' He saw the way Michael was looking at him. 'Not me! Pass it on to a financial management firm. Let them decide where the gold goes.'

'A hundred metric tonnes,' Michael said with exasperation. 'A hundred tonnes of gold, and it's worthless. We sell it on the Earthly, we drive the price of gold down and hurt ourselves and the world economy; something we're sworn to protect. We keep it, it's doing nothing. What the hell was Greg thinking?'

'He was planning to employ stones to fashion it into high-end jewellery and sell it for celestial jade,' Rohan said.

Michael leaned back. 'Clever. Good plan, turning gold that costs us nothing into jade that's worth something here on the Celestial. So what happened? Why isn't the storehouse full of jade instead of gold?'

'The stones died. The demons kidnapped them and experimented on them and too many of them died.'

'And the Grandmother of All the Rocks took the survivors home with her in disgust. I see.' Michael sighed and rubbed his hands over his face. 'Can we spare half-a-dozen people to create a fake gold mine?'

'You know the answer to that.'

'Hmm.' Michael contacted the head of the Seraglio Elite Guard. *William?*

Rohan heard it and grinned. He knew what was coming.

*Fuck off I'm on my break.*

Rohan's grin widened.

Michael ignored William's griping. *I know, I saw Dad go down there. Are any of the wives experts at financial management?*

*You are referring to the wives of our father the White Tiger, yes?*

*I am.*

*And you're seriously asking me this question?*

*Oh come on, there have to be one or two he met while he was in the city …*

*Our father does not favour women with brains.*

Rohan interrupted. *Wrong. Women with brains do not favour our father.*

*Number Two has a valid point,* William said. *Any woman with half a brain would steer well clear of him.*

*It was worth a try, we have financial issues and someone with access to the current trading figures would be very useful.*

*Hold on,* William said, and was quiet for a moment. *Hey, leave it with me for a while. I'm dating a dragon who does that sort of thing in the Eastern Palace, he may have access to the info you need. I'll see if he can help.*

*Thanks, man, you're the best.*

*Oh shit, I hear screaming. Someone missed her turn with Dad. Later.*

Michael sighed. 'Clarissa would know what to do.'

'Michael, Clarissa's not the solution to everything.'

'She is to me.' Michael closed the budget folder. 'Leave the gold where it is until William gets back to us. Trickle sell it as we always do, but we need to find another source of income – real Celestial income, not this Earthly crap – soon, because we all know what's coming.'

'Is it really?'

'It is.'

Rohan studied him intensely. 'How much can you see?'

'Since I was promoted to Number One, more than I want to. War, Rohan. War with demonkind – bloody, unrelenting, and brutal. There's a good chance the Celestial will lose and we'll all end up being tortured in the tenth level of Hell for a long time.'

'How long a long time?'

'Long enough to regret accepting Immortality, brother.'

The next day Michael was going through the metal commodity prices on the internet when Rohan came in and flopped into the seat across the desk from him, his grin wide.

'Anything useful for me, or you just here to be decorative?' Michael said without looking away from the screen.

'We found a big nest. Really big nest. Hundreds of them. Want to come help?'

Michael dropped the mouse and pushed himself away from the desk, then stopped and wheeled himself back again. 'No. I'm too busy. You can handle it. How many are you taking with you?'

Rohan's voice went sly. 'There'll be Mothers, Michael.'

'Dad would kill me.'

'Dad's in the harem. Come on, man, you really need to blow off some steam and if we run into more than half-a-dozen Mothers, it could get hairy. We may seriously need you.'

'Where is it?'

'Under Bezeklik.'

'Where's that?'

'Called Bozhikeli in Putonghua.'

'Never heard of it.'

Rohan let his breath out in a long hiss.

'I'm half-American and grew up in Hong Kong,' Michael said. 'If you want someone more local as Number One, feel free to take the job yourself.'

'Yeah, sure. Good try.'

Michael turned back to the computer, googled Bezeklik and went through to the Wikipedia article. 'The Thousand-Buddha Caves?'

'Those ones. Hardly any Buddhas left, though, archaeologists stole most of them in the early twentieth century. Not much there but the caves – and a massive nest complex underneath. Our scouts estimate that the nest entrance is as old as the caves themselves.'

'Fifth to fourteenth century. Damn, that nest is *old*.'

'We're looking at seriously huge Mothers in there. Hopefully some Dukes as well. Should be a fun field trip.'

'We shouldn't be wasting our time on Mothers and Dukes, we should be targeting military thralls that we can tame and add to our defensive army.'

'Well, plenty of them too. Of course. But this breeding colony will be producing high-level war demons and if we shut it down, it could gut their military forces.'

'That's halfway across the continent and on the Earthly Plane. I don't have a whole day to waste doing this, Rohan.'

'Big Mothers, Michael.'

'You can handle it.'

'And Dukes. And lots of military thralls to tame and present to Dad to add to his own army – you'll be his favourite son for ages. Come on, man, it'll be great fun. You haven't drawn a weapon in anger for weeks.'

Michael turned to argue with Rohan, and hesitated when he saw his brother's desperation. 'You really think you'll need me?'

Rohan grimaced. 'To be honest? Yeah. I could only round up fifteen Horsemen with enough training and none of them are Immortal. We may be a little out of our depth here, man. The scout says there's some really weird shit happening down there – the scout that returned, that is. Three were stationed in that area and only one came back, and he's really disturbed by what he saw, and his memory seems to be wiped. The therapists are using hypnosis to help him recall what happened, but there's something ... wrong.'

Michael held his hand out over the desk and his sword, the White Tiger, appeared on it. He stood and picked it up. 'How are you planning to travel there?'

'We'll borrow one of Dad's choppers.'

'All right, count me in.'

Rohan's expression filled with relief.

'But you're writing the report for Dad when we get back,' Michael said.

'Sure, but I could copy the contents of the *People's Daily*, hand it to him as a report, and he'd never know, because he never reads them.'

'I know that – I've done it too.'

The helicopter landed twenty kilometres away from the caves and Michael and Rohan quietly teleported the squad closer. They walked along the road to the tourist car park, a flat gravel area above the little valley that held the caves. The usual tourist-trap city had been set up, with camel rides and paid photo opportunities, but it was just on nightfall and all the stalls were closed.

Rohan signalled a couple of soldiers and made them invisible to reconnaissance. The rest of the squad waited quietly until they returned and reappeared.

'No surveillance we can see,' one of the scouts said. 'No guards, no cameras, no civilians. All clear.'

Michael gestured for them to move out. 'Number Two on point. I'll bring up the rear.'

The squad moved into formation and went down the steps to the caves, which were set into the side of a river valley only a hundred metres across. The yellow earth formed a steep buttress on the other side, and the only greenery was some straggly trees and shrubs clinging to the bottom of the valley and the water from the river. There was no other habitation for kilometres, and nothing grew for a great distance on either side of the little valley. Several archways carved into the rock of the valley wall led away from a wide flat area that overlooked the water.

Rohan led them into one of the entrances and through the narrow corridors. The cave complex wasn't large; each opening led to a narrow corridor that went three metres into the hillside, ended with an altar, then looped back out again. Some held brightly coloured Buddhist murals but most were bare rock, scarred where the frescoes had been chiselled away.

'The German archaeologists took them,' Rohan said as he led the team through the corridor. 'Took them back to Germany where they'd be safe from the bloodthirsty local savages. Most of the paintings were destroyed when the museum holding them in Germany was bombed during a war between the bloodthirsty local savages.'

'I believe it,' Michael said. He put on a fake British accent. 'But our wars are different. When good white men go to war it's all about honour and valour, none of this Oriental savagery.' He saw the way Rohan was looking at him. 'I know, I know, I'm one of them. So where's the nest entrance?'

'Of course it's the altar.' Rohan gestured towards the wall, which held a fresco of an obviously European Bodhisattva; white skin and blue eyes. 'I didn't know there were gweilo Buddhas.'

Michael shrugged. 'The Wudang Energy Master is a Taoist Immortal. It could even be a picture of her.'

'You're right, it does look like her.' Rohan checked around. 'All clear. Looks like I was right and they weren't expecting us.'

'You're right about surprise; I'm right about the Bodhisattva. Something has to go seriously wrong now.'

'I hear you. On point.' Rohan walked through the wall and Michael waited for the rest of the squad to enter, again guarding the rear.

The tunnels on the other side looked exactly the

same, but they hadn't been damaged. Tan earth walls led up to an arched roof and more frescoes covered the walls. Michael stopped and studied one: it showed a group of Buddhist pilgrims, some Asian and some European, wearing saffron robes and carrying lotus flowers. A description was inscribed under each figure, saying where they were from and their humanitarian achievements.

'This isn't what you'd expect to find in a nest entrance,' Michael said.

'It changes further along, according to the intel,' Rohan said. 'When they first entered, the scouts thought they'd just reached a part of the caves that had been hidden by an Immortal.' He gestured with his head. 'Come and see.'

The end of the tunnel opened into a large underground room with a domed ceiling, twenty metres across, decorated with more Buddhist frescoes. Panels within the dome held depictions of the twenty-eight Buddhas, from the most ancient to the Maitreya Buddha Yet to Come. The walls were still the same tan earth, but it was buffed and polished to a sheen that made it appear to be shining gold. The frescoes hadn't faded with the years; they still glowed bright as jewels.

'I am so glad the archaeologists never made it in here,' Michael said, turning to see the contents of the room with awe. 'After we clean this nest out we must do something about preserving this.'

'The best method would probably be to lock it up,' Rohan said, standing next to him and studying the brilliant ceiling. 'Take a complete survey and digital record, and then make sure that nobody ever enters again.'

'When we return, remind me to liaise with the Phoenix's people about preservation,' Michael said. 'They're the materials specialists, they should have some good ideas, and they're deeply protective of the Buddhist legacy.'

'Sir.'

Michael glanced sharply at Rohan, who was still studying the ceiling. He nodded and turned to the rest of the squad. 'Be very careful not to touch anything. Let's go.'

As they proceeded down the tunnel, the frescoes changed. The colours shifted from brilliant blues and golds to red and black, and showed scenes of battle and conquest instead of peaceful offering and celebration. Michael stopped when he saw a fresco that didn't show a Buddha or devotee at all – it depicted a Snake Mother in True Form holding a screaming human to her impossibly wide mouth. A red inscription below the Mother said, *Honoured Number Sixteen who brought more than a hundred humans for us to play with. Their skulls and bones adorn our nest and bring joy to our hearts.*

Michael sniffed the air; the earthy scent from the tunnel walls was strong, but there was a definite odour of nest from up ahead; death and decay.

Rohan nodded. 'Now it gets intense.'

As they travelled down the tunnel, the frescoes petered out to nothing and the walls darkened from gold to black. They descended steeply, the floor sometimes slippery with moisture. They all felt it at the same time and stopped. Michael worked his way through the group to Rohan at the head.

Michael sent his senses through the tunnels ahead of them and he and Rohan shared a look. There were at least three hundred small- to mid-sized demons ahead, with a group of twenty or so really big ones – either Duke or Mother level. Michael studied his own squad – he and Rohan were the only Immortals present – and nearly ordered them out.

*What did the intel say about the level of training?*
Michael asked Rohan.

*The demons don't appear to be trained, they are big but not warriors. This nest has never been attacked so they're complacent.*

Michael worked out the numbers and came up slightly positive on his own side. They could take them; and removing this many huge breeding Mothers from the Horde of Hell would give the Celestial forces a serious tactical advantage in the war to come. It could mean the difference between an improbable victory and a very likely Celestial defeat.

He nodded once, sharply, and sent an order out to the troop. *Me on point; Number Two on rear guard. Have your weapons out and ready.*

The rest of the squad drew their swords, and Michael pulled out his own and held it. Rohan moved to the back of the group to guard the rear, and Michael made them all invisible and led them to the end of the tunnel.

The tunnel opened into one of the largest nest chambers he had ever seen, short of the chamber containing the highest level Mothers in the centre of Hell. The cavern stretched higher and further than he could see, and the air was full of the dank odour of the demon inhabitants. Dry slithering indicated that the Mothers were on the move – they hadn't settled for the night yet – and Michael led the squad along the left wall, masking their sound and scent.

*On my word, take them out one by one, pull them to the side and finish them,* he said. *Backs to the wall and defensive formation when we're discovered. Try to quietly remove as many as you can before they raise the alarm.*

He led the group to the edge of the populated area of the nest, where floor hollows three metres across sat at five-metre intervals. Each hollow was claimed by a Mother for her eggs. One of the Mothers was reclining in her hollow nearby and Michael led the group towards her, still keeping them silent.

The air exploded with loud bangs and the head of the soldier next to Michael burst in a gush of blood and brains and shattered bone that hit him with piercing splinters. Michael ducked and moved to the side; a group of Mothers armed with automatic firearms had been hiding behind their sisters and now raised their human front ends on their snake back halves to let loose on the squad. The soldiers fell, their bodies shredded by the force of the bullets that crashed into them. As the only other Immortal there, Rohan was fast enough to block bullets with his blade; but he was overwhelmed, half his head blew out, and his body disappeared.

Michael sent a blast of energy into the middle of the Mothers and the two centre ones were destroyed. He needed to find cover and there wasn't any. He snapped chi armour around himself, but it wouldn't hold for long. He sent another blast of energy into the Mothers but these resisted it: too big. He changed to shen energy, the flaming energy of his half-god soul, and destroyed them.

The chi armour faded. The Mothers moved faster than he could see and surrounded him. He needed to open his Inner Eye to destroy them but he was struck on the back of the head.

Someone held his arms and was dragging him, on his behind, through the dirt. His head was splitting and he wanted badly to throw up. The nausea overcame him and he gagged, then spat some bile out to one side. He looked up to see what was pulling him, and only saw a confused jumble of brown and black. He collapsed and retched again.

They stopped dragging him and he peered up at them. Two really big Mothers in human form towered over him, holding one arm each. They were exceptionally tall, slim, gorgeous women – supermodel gorgeous. One appeared Indian and the other looked Thai. Michael's gut heaved again but he managed to avoid vomiting.

The Mothers released his arms and he fell to the floor on his back. He stared at the ceiling; it was the arched room with the Buddhist frescoes. One of the Mothers kicked him in the side and he grunted.

'Cut that out, Dad wants him alive and in one piece.'

Someone crouched over him, blocking the view of the ceiling. It was another big demon, a Duke in female human form. She lifted his eyelids and shone a light into his eyes. He winced at the pain that seared through his head.

'He'll live,' she said. 'Well done.'

They pulled at his left arm and he tried to jerk it away but failed. Something stung the inside of his elbow – a needle. They were drugging him, and he was too weakened and disoriented to fight it.

'Take him through,' the Duke said. They grabbed his arms and dragged him as it all faded away.

His head was bumping painfully against something. He was sprawled, half-sitting, across a seat and bouncing – he was in a car. He pulled himself upright and nearly threw up again. His head pounded and he was deliriously thirsty. He wondered how much time had passed.

'Take it easy,' a male voice said. 'They hit you way too hard. Can you see?'

Michael opened his eyes and peered at the demon speaking to him. He was in a van, facing the back, and it lurched again; the nausea roiled up and he looked around for something to throw up into.

'Sick,' he gasped out.

'Oh,' the demon said, and quickly passed him a plastic shopping bag.

These things usually had holes in them but Michael couldn't stop the gush of bile and stomach acid. He retched a few more times, then bent over his knees, trying to settle his stomach and overcome the pounding in his head. His hands automatically tied a knot in the top of the bag and he dropped it onto the floor of the van.

'Combination of a heroin overdose and concussion – unfortunately you'll survive, Prince Michael, even if it feels like you won't,' the demon said.

'Don't want to,' Michael mumbled. 'Please, kill me now.'

'What, and miss the opportunity my father's about to give you? He's going to take you into the European Heavens,' the demon said with amusement.

Michael's head shot up to study the demon, and he realised with a shock that it was the Demon King's Number One Son himself. He was in male human form with slicked-back blond hair and wearing a grey silk suit. Michael glanced out the window; they were travelling through the desert at highway speed, with no other vehicles around for any distance. He winced at the light and looked away.

'Why would he take me to the European Heavens?' Michael said. The Asian Shen had been trying for years to contact their European counterparts. If he could enter the European Heavens, he could discover why the European Shen were absolutely quiet and didn't respond to any of the Asian Shen's overtures. The fact that the Asian Demon King could travel there was seriously disturbing and this was a brilliant opportunity to find out exactly what was going on.

'You're the biggest son of the White Tiger,' the

demon said. 'But better than that, you're half-European and they may talk to you. Your mother was descended from the European Serpent people. Do you know about them?'

'There were Serpent people in Europe?'

'It's a long story.' Number One smiled and covered it by rubbing his mouth. 'Suffice to say your mother was just as much demon as she was human. Considering what your father is, you should be glad you were Raised to Immortality the old-fashioned way and didn't attempt to take the Elixir – it would probably do the same thing to you that it did to your dear old mum.'

Michael inhaled sharply. 'You know why my mother exploded?'

'I just told you, didn't I? She was a human-demon mix. So are you.' The demon studied him carefully. 'You and me together could probably take my father down, you know. I could rule in Hell, and you could go home to your girlfriend.'

'You think I'd work with you after what you did to her? She's a blind paraplegic with serious PTSD after what you demons did to her. She's a broken husk of what she used to be.' His voice thickened. 'She thought I'd be her knight in shining armour and ride in to rescue her, and I never did because they told me she was dead.'

'It was Dad that did it to her, not me. Even more reason for you to kill him, eh? I want him gone as well – he's negotiating with the European demons. Those bastards will end up controlling the Asian demons, the same way they colonised and controlled Asia during the Opium Wars. I won't let that happen, and you can help me stop him. We can work together.'

Michael hesitated. The demon was right. Michael also knew in personal and excruciating detail exactly how much success he could expect if he made a pact with demons.

'I'll just go check out the European Heavens, thanks. Sounds like fun.'

'Don't let them take any genetic material,' the demon said. 'If they give you a sample jar, whatever you do, don't fill it. They want to make copies of you.'

Michael winced. More copies. This Demon King made copies of humans, demons and Celestials and using them as spies, and only the Dark Lord himself could distinguish some of them. A copy of Michael could be inserted into his father's palace undetected, and provide the demons with limitless information on the Celestial plans. Once he had enough intelligence, Michael needed to blow his brains out as quickly as he could and go home to Asia.

The demon nodded. 'If it comes to a choice of killing yourself or giving them a genetic sample, choose death.'

'Why are you helping me?'

Number One leaned back in his seat and smiled. 'You're really asking me that?'

'I won't help you take down your father.'

'Just by talking to me, Prince Michael, you already are.' The demon glanced out the window. 'From here you'll go on a private jet. Dad and Francis are in Europe waiting for you.'

'Who's Francis?'

'King of the European Demons,' Number One said with venom. 'He has seduced our King with tales of power and is planning to rule us all.' The van stopped and he slid the door open. 'We have similar goals, Prince Michael. Both of us want to see the Asian King taken down. I can't come to the European Heavens, they're too far from my Centre. Only Dad and half-European demons can do it, with Francis's help. I'm counting on you to help me stop the Europeans from enslaving us all.' He took Michael's arm. 'Pretend to still be drugged and dazed, so they won't wonder why you haven't escaped. Come around on the plane – by then it will be too late for you to escape.'

Michael half-closed his eyes and leaned on Number One as he was led from the van to the small waiting business jet.

He didn't have time to see where he was before he was dragged up the stairs into the private jet and the door closed behind him. He kept his eyes half-closed as a demon Duke in female human form pushed him into a large comfortable seat.

Her presence remained in front of him for a long moment, then she spoke. 'You're pretending to be unconscious. Can you speak, Prince Michael?'

His limbs were still like lead and he didn't need to fake the struggle to sit upright and be fully conscious. 'Huh?'

'Let me know when you're able to talk.'

'I can talk,' he said, his words slurred.

She turned and sat in the chair across from him, and waved towards the back of the plane. 'Can I get you anything? There's food and drinks back there. Dad says you're to be treated like the royalty you are.'

Michael pulled himself out of the chair and staggered to the back of the plane.

'Let me,' she said, trying to help him, but he pushed her away.

He pulled a bottle of water out of the fridge, then went back to his seat, fell into it and had a long drink. He tasted the bitterness and spat the water back into the bottle, but had already consumed most of it.

'You didn't need to do that,' he said. 'I want to see the European Heavens. I won't try to escape.' He looked inside himself, studying the way the opium was slowing his nervous system, and tried to reverse the effect, but he had been drugged and bashed too many times to retain the concentration he needed. His eyes closed by themselves. 'Stop … drugging …'

His head was still pounding when the loud roar of the jets woke him a long time later. He remained completely still and attempted to contact his father. Nothing.

Rohan. Nothing. William. Nothing. What the hell?

'Are you awake there, Highness?' the demon said.

Michael pulled his sluggish body upright. 'Do you have anything to drink that isn't drugged?'

The demon passed him a bottle of energy drink; probably a good idea to have some sugar after all he'd been through. He popped the top and took a sip; it tasted clean so he drank it quickly, nearly giving himself a brain freeze from the cold. He took a few gasping breaths, drank some more, and rested his head in his hands. 'You wouldn't have any Panadol as well, would you?'

'Sorry, things like that don't work on us,' the demon said. 'Just to warn you; touch the wall of the plane.'

Michael ran his hand over the surface of the wall and then snapped it back; the wall of the plan was so full of anguish and suffering that it hurt. He'd heard about this, but never experienced it in person. The wall had been painted with the ground remains of stone Shen. Intelligent, sentient creatures had died in terror and pain, then been powdered and painted on the walls. The surface echoed with their screams, and fear emanated from it. No wonder there was no communication through that.

'Can't teleport either,' the demon said. 'Nifty, eh? The pilot's human; if you break out of the plane to escape you'll kill him.'

'I won't escape. I want to see the European Heavens,' Michael said.

'Oh,' the demon said. 'Information gathering?'

'Of course.' Michael studied the wall of the plane. 'How many stones died to make this?'

'On this plane alone, thirty-three stone Shen,' the demon said. 'We're running out of them.'

Michael shifted back in his seat and took another drink. Now that he was getting some carbs and rehydrating, his half-Shen metabolism was recovering quickly. He winced as he remembered what had happened. He'd led fifteen of his mortal brothers straight into a trap that had killed all of them. He was a complete failure as Number One Son and as soon as he was home he needed to resign the position. In the meantime he could find out what the demons were up to in Europe, so the sortie wasn't a complete failure. Nothing would bring his brothers back, though. He wiped his hand over his eyes, then straightened to talk to the demon.

'Can you tell me about the European Heavens?' he said.

'Wait,' the demon said. She grinned. 'The King said I can tell you anything you want to know, and thanks you for your cooperation.'

'Aren't the European Shen pissed that you are there?'

'There aren't any. They're all gone. Fortunately Dad has a way with energy and managed to break into the European Heavens, and everything was right there waiting for us.'

'Where did all the Shen go?'

The Duke shrugged. 'Dad will tell you more about it; I'm as confused as you are. You Celestials are completely beyond me sometimes. Waste all your time looking after people who don't appreciate you when you could be living it up and enjoying yourself.'

'I hear you man,' Michael said with amusement that he hoped sounded genuine. 'Managing my father's palace is a pain in the ass and I wish I'd never taken the job. Absolutely no appreciation whatsoever for the difficult job I do.'

The demon shot a piercing glance at Michael. Michael grinned in response. The demon smiled and wiggled further down in her seat to watch him under her eyelashes. 'I'd appreciate you,' she purred.

'One-woman man, sorry,' Michael said, his grin growing wry. 'And your dad destroyed that one woman's life.'

The demon sat up straighter and looked out the window. 'We'll see about that,' she said softly.

They landed at a tiny airfield and the Duke opened the door for Michael. The deserted airstrip was surrounded by fields of low bushes, cold and windswept. He shivered – really cold; they must be in the far northern part of Europe. He didn't know how long he'd been travelling and had no idea what time zone he was in, but the sun was low in the west.

The minute he stepped out of the plane he broadcast his presence, hoping someone nearby would pick him up – backup would be handy.

Nothing.

'We're in the middle of nowhere,' the demon said with amusement.

*One?* his father said.

*I'm in Europe. They're taking me to the European Heavens. Send someone to my location —*

*Where?*

*I have no idea. North. It's cold and sparsely populated. Can you locate me?*

A van pulled up and they bundled him into the back of it. Once again his transmissions were blocked – the interior was covered in the stone paint as well.

'It's about an hour to the gateway, then you'll see how the Europeans did Heaven,' the Duke said. 'It's truly breathtaking, and Dad's made sure that nobody's defaced it.' She smiled wryly. 'He has an appreciation for the finer things, most cultured King we've had in centuries. Sensitive, sophisticated and completely ruthless, we're all crazy about him. He's the best.'

They drove through flat fields of flowers, and the windmills identified the country – it had to be the Netherlands. Michael had never been there before and didn't recognise any of the landmarks. The houses grew closer together and the buildings became taller as they drove into an urban area with tree-lined wide roads.

'Is this Amsterdam?' Michael asked the demon as he peered through the window and saw a group of houses that were cubes sitting on pillars – but sitting on their points. 'Whoa. How do they live in them?'

'No, Rotterdam,' the demon said. 'It was razed to the ground, every building destroyed during World War Two. After the war, the city gave the architects free rein to do what they liked. Some very interesting architectural experiments were a result. These cube houses are famous – probably for being as impractical as they are unique.'

'Are the floors sloping at an angle?'

'No, each little house is three storeys with a flat floor and sloping walls. When you go inside it's not that strange, and they're quite roomy. One of them is open for tourists to see, maybe one day you'll be able to bring your family.'

'I don't have a family,' Michael said, watching the cubes go past.

'You have a father and many brothers and

sisters.'

'Half of them wouldn't notice if I were to die here, and the other half would cheer,' Michael said. 'The only family who really cared for me is dead.' They travelled a few more kilometres between unremarkable houses and along a canal, until the van pulled into the back of a very old gothic cathedral and parked. 'I thought you said the city was razed?'

'The gateway was the only building that survived. The locals thought it was a miracle.'

'The church is the gateway?'

'Of course it is – an ancient holy site. You should see the photographs – the entire city flattened and this cathedral still standing.' The demon opened the van and gestured for Michael to exit. 'Please don't cause us any trouble, Prince Michael, and we'll treat you with honour and respect. Come with us and see the European Heavens.'

'I won't give you any trouble. I want to see,' Michael said. *I'm in Rotterdam. The gateway is the cathedral. I'm going up to the European Heavens.*

'I don't think anyone will be able to make it here in time to stop us,' the demon said. 'Warn them that we're waiting for them if they try to come?'

*And there's an ambush waiting here.*

*Understood,* his father said. *Try to keep in touch. I'm sending Three and Four to back you up.*

*Acknowledged. Going in now.*

The interior of the cathedral was one huge room, with Gothic pointed arches high above them. The Asian Demon King was sitting in one of the pews at the front, near the elaborate gold-plated altar. The Duke guided Michael to the King, bowed to him, then stood silently at the end of the row.

'Sit, Prince Michael, sit,' the King said, gesturing.

Michael sat carefully just out of reach of the King

and studied him. He was in his male Chinese human form: fair, almost transparent, skin, shoulder-length maroon hair and maroon jeans and a black polo shirt. His face was classically handsome – he could be a movie star – but the effect was marred by the cruelty in his blood-coloured eyes.

'I have a gift for you in the European Heavens,' the King said. 'You have been systematically and ruthlessly lied to by the Celestial bureaucracy for years, and I'm here to set things right.'

'What is it?'

The King raised one hand slightly where it had been resting on the back of the pew. 'Better to show you. We'll take you up immediately, but I have to warn you about the gravity first.'

'The gravity?'

'Within the walls of the city of Murias, the gravity is only two-thirds earth normal. Weirdest damn thing you've ever seen. Or felt.'

Michael hesitated then said, 'Why?'

'My researchers think it's for aesthetic reasons.'

'Aesthetic reasons? To make it *pretty*?'

'Absolutely. You'll understand when you see. But be warned; tread lightly, because you'll push yourself higher and faster under the weaker gravity with no effort whatsoever. I know you can fly, and for the first few days it might be better to travel around that way instead.' The King hoisted himself and gestured towards the altar. 'If you'll come with me, Highness, let's have a reunion.'

They stepped through the gateway onto a causeway, twenty metres wide and hundreds long, suspended above the brilliantly green forest surrounding the city. Michael's stomach leaped and lurched, and he felt the lightness – the gravity really was reduced.

Glass and silver spires soared to the heavens

around the causeway, appearing much too slender and tall to stand – and obviously only able to exist in the reduced gravity. The floor of the causeway was tiled, each tile a rich peacock blue and forty centimetres across. The deep blue looked like it was under a thick layer of transparent glass but the surface was somehow non-slip and easy to stand on.

The spires were also made of glass; panels of different shapes, some frosted and others clear, with the occasional jewel-like coloured piece, and all set into a fine decorative metal framework. The metal had a white patina over it, exactly the same way freshly polished silver did. Michael reached out with his metal connection and saw with wonder that the towers really were silver – a complex amalgam of silver, mercury and a variety of other metals that made them strong and tarnish proof.

He turned on the spot, seeing the soft sunset of the Celestial sky reflecting through the glass of the towers and the sides of the causeway and mirrored in the tiles beneath his feet. The Demon King gestured for Michael to join him at the edge of the causeway to see the view. Michael took a step and lurched – he'd gone three times further than he intended and landed clumsily. He took a few hesitant, gentle steps. It was reasonably easy to adjust to the reduced gravity and he strode more confidently, moving metres with each step. Eventually he took three big strides and jumped, sailing over the King's head and off the causeway. He grinned ruefully at how far he'd gone, stopped his fall into the gardens below, and flew back onto the causeway.

When he was standing at the edge of the causeway next to the King, he looked around at the city below. It spread for kilometres before them, with large halls and multi-storey buildings, again impossibly tall and slender in construction, and decorated with more towers, some joined together with dizzyingly high bridges and walkways. Terraces along the sides of the buildings held gardens and boxes containing healthy green foliage and brightly coloured flowers, mostly blue and white.

'Welcome to Murias, the Silver City,' the King said.

'Are these floor tiles glass?' Michael said. 'How did they keep them in such good condition? There's not a single scratch on them.'

'Yes, they're glass. The people of this city were experts in manipulating glass; most of the construction is glass and metal and very little else. No concrete anywhere in this city. There's tales that some of the European Shen even wore armour of glass.'

The technology was beyond anything that Michael knew of in the Asian Heavens and he needed to uncover more of the city's secrets. 'So where to now?'

'There's someone you need to see.' The Demon King turned and gestured back the way they'd come, towards the Celestial analogue of the cathedral on the Earthly Plane.

The building on the end of the causeway was five times higher than it was wide, and again decorated with the impossibly tall spires. The construction was the silver amalgam and glass, but all the glass was coloured to produce a reflective rainbow that shimmered before them.

The Demon King led Michael to the cathedral and they entered, Michael still struggling to keep his walk to a decent pace and not cover the distance in huge steps that unbalanced him. The floor was black glass that reflected the coloured walls and ceiling to give the impression they were walking on water. The interior soared two hundred metres above them in a single vast empty space. There was no religious iconography that Michael could recognise; the building held long benches on either side with a single throne at the far end. A round stained-glass rose window was high on the wall behind the throne, showing a group of noble-looking European people on foot and horseback, wearing robes and gold jewellery.

'Parliament,' the King said. He gestured with his head. 'The palace on the other side appears to be the Emperor's residence, and we've put them there.'

'Put who there?' Michael said, studying the intricate silver filigree between the glass panels high above them. 'How the hell do they clean the windows up there?'

'This city worked much the same way your Celestial Palace does: there was a single spirit of the city with many servitors that worked for the city itself. The city came complete with fairy servants that could fly, and they maintained everything.' The King gestured again. 'This way, Highness.'

They went through a double doorway three metres wide and five high to a terrace that overlooked more terraces of gardens and fountains with a spired gothic mansion on the other side, glittering in the sun.

The King led Michael down the stairs between the garden boxes. 'First: that wasn't your mother who exploded at her coronation as Empress of the West. It was a copy I'd made, and was too demon to accept the Elixir of Immortality. It killed her.'

Michael remained silent. The King was obviously lying.

'Five years ago, you agreed to her spending a week with me in exchange for information. I replaced her with a copy all that time ago and I've been holding her ever since.'

'My mother passed through the Courts of Hell. Judge Pao told me that she wasn't found Worthy, and he's the one who judged her.'

'They lied to you, they didn't want you to know that everybody had been fooled by a copy.' The King stopped at the bottom of the stairs and gazed at the garden. 'Second: well, you can judge for yourself.' He gestured towards the blonde woman sitting on a park bench.

It was his mother, Rhonda. She leaped to her feet when she saw them.

'Michael!' she shrieked, and ran to him. She pulled him into a huge hug and kissed him on both cheeks, then pulled back to wipe tears from her eyes. 'It is you. The King promised you'd come and I didn't believe him, but here you are.' She embraced him again. 'Thank you, George, thank you so much.' She noticed that Michael wasn't returning her affection and moved back to talk to him. 'It's me, Mikey, it really is. I spent a week with the King to prove to everybody that I was confident about marrying your father, and he never let me go. George has been holding me prisoner —'

'I prefer the term "guest", my Lady,' the Demon King said.

'Prisoner,' Rhonda continued. 'But it was okay once —'

'Michael!'

Michael's heart leapt. It was Clarissa. Clarissa, unhurt, undamaged, bursting with life and energy. She ran – almost floated – through the gardens to him and threw herself into his arms and he held her close and kissed her hair. It was her: her fragrance, her feel; the soft sound of her sweet voice. It was *her*.

'You are breaking my heart, George,' he said over the top of her head.

'No, Michael, this is your real fiancée. We replaced her ages ago. The copy was in the lab being experimented on and didn't take it well at all; much too fragile. This is your real mother and your real fiancée and you can take them home with you.'

'We can go home?' Rhonda said, full of hope.

'Michael needs to do a simple job for me, then you can all go home unharmed.'

'I won't betray the Celestial. Not for anything,' Michael said.

'You don't need to. Spend some time with your mother and girlfriend, and I'll come back tomorrow and we can talk about the job you need to do. It doesn't involve any betrayal of the Celestial, violence or killing. We just want the secret of the gravity, and we're hoping that as a half-European demigod, the spirit of the city will talk to you and explain how it's done.' The King linked his hands behind his back. 'Settle in. Spend time with your family. Enjoy the citadel, and I'll be back tomorrow to discuss terms for the release of all three of you.' He turned and headed back towards the parliament building.

Rhonda and Clarissa took one of Michael's arms each and led him into the mansion. It was constructed of glass and silver, the same as the rest of the city. The doors opened into a hall that swept two storeys up to the clear glass roof that showed the darkening sky above them. The walls on either side were decorated with huge portraits of noble-looking men and women in embroidered robes similar to what Rhonda and Clarissa were wearing; rulers of the past. Stairs in front of them led to a landing that sat around three sides of the hall.

'It's a shame that the European Shen aren't here any more,' Clarissa said. 'They look kind.'

'How long have you two been here?' Michael said.

'We'll tell you over dinner,' Rhonda said, dragging him to a set of double doors. The doors led through to a long dining hall with a large rectangular table set

Western-style with silver candelabras and fine china along its length. 'The demons have been looking after us, but we've still been prisoners. I hope you can sort something out with the Demon King to take us home.'

He followed them to the end of the table, still dazed and delighted to be back with them. He knew damn well they weren't real, but they were there and that was enough for him. They sat on either side at the end of the table and gestured for him to take a seat between them. It was like one of the dreams he'd had for many years, where all the horrible things hadn't really happened and he was back with them; but this was reality. They were warm and real – and demon copies. The pain in his chest was like a knife through his heart and he needed to run and hide and weep for hours.

Instead he took a sip of the water from the crystal goblet in front of him, his hand shaking. The glass shimmered in the light from the floor-to-ceiling windows and he studied it, trying to pull himself together. Pine sprigs and pine cones were etched into its surface in such meticulous detail that it was a work of art. Every item on the table was intricately adorned, from the pine motif on the porcelain to the silver pine needles and pine cones decorating the candelabras. The candle-holders had no candles in them; instead long, six-sided natural crystals provided a warm and welcoming glow, enough light for everything to be clearly visible. More crystals sat in stands on the sides of the room.

He raised his hands, one to each woman. 'Take my hands.'

They took his hands. He lowered his head and concentrated.

Nothing happened.

'Did you just try to teleport us out?' Clarissa said.

Michael released their hands and nodded.

'It was worth a try, Mikey,' Rhonda said with compassion. 'Can you go by yourself?'

'I won't leave you,' he said.

Demon servants came out from a side door and placed plates in front of them. They held traditional Western-style appetisers: smoked fish with a white sauce he didn't recognise. He stuck his fork into it and held it in front of his eyes, suspicious.

Rhonda and Clarissa weren't as hesitant; they cut into the fish and tasted it with obvious enjoyment. He took a small bite from his fork and nearly choked on the smoky, intense flavour. It was excellent. He had a couple more bites then turned to Rhonda and studied her. She appeared about five years older, which matched the time since she'd agreed to be the guest of the King; the Demon King's other copies hadn't aged, so there was a slight, maddening, chance that she was real. Clarissa seemed the same as she always had. The two women he loved most in the world, alive and real and sitting beside him. Rhonda's fair complexion and blonde hair contrasted against Clarissa's Chinese black hair and perfect skin, and seeing the two of them together was more joy than his heart could hold.

If the Demon King's task wasn't too difficult, he could complete it, take them home, and sort it all out later. Back in the Asian Heavens, he could find out for sure whether they were copies or not. He just needed to try not to get too attached to them in the meantime. Clarissa smiled and his heart ached with love for her.

'So tell me how you came to be here, and how long you've been here,' he said, trying to push the feeling aside.

They opened their mouths together, then both smiled and shared a look. Clarissa gestured towards Rhonda, and Rhonda nodded and spoke.

'The Demon King was a perfect gentleman for

the week I stayed with him. He never did more than try to talk me out of remarrying your father. The days seemed to blur past, and I wasn't really aware of time, but I was sure the week had finished and he kept saying the last day would be "tomorrow". I gave him two days and then demanded to be taken home, and that's when he moved me from the guest house to another villa that was effectively a prison. He hasn't hurt me – in fact he's treated me well, and promised, over and over for years now, that one day you would come to take me home.' She reached out to squeeze his hand. 'And here you are, finally.' She brushed tears out of her eyes. 'It's been breaking my heart to think about leaving you all alone.'

'Yes, have you been all right?' Clarissa said, her voice soft with sympathy. 'Both of us left you.' She smiled. 'But we're back together now and after you do this little job for the King we can go home.'

Michael opened his mouth to tell them that they were probably demon copies – and couldn't do it. 'Well, I was really angry when you turned up alive after the Dark Lord told me you were dead,' he said to Clarissa. 'I left the job in his household and took the position as my father's Number One Son.'

'You're the Tiger's Number One now?' Rhonda said sharply.

Michael nodded.

'Good,' she said. 'About time you two finally sorted out your differences. I'll have a proper family to return to, a husband and a son.'

'With more than a hundred other wives as competition,' Michael said.

Rhonda waved it away. 'Nobody will question my fitness to hold the position of Empress of the West, and there are a few things around the Western Palace that could do with a definite update. I cannot wait to go home and start working with you and the Tiger to bring the entire complex into the twenty-first century. You can help if you like, Clarissa, after you've married Michael.'

'I'd love to,' Clarissa said. 'I'm sure the finances could do with a serious overhaul.'

'You have no idea,' Michael said.

'There's a wedding we need to plan as well,' Rhonda said, bright with pleasure. 'And this time nothing will go wrong.'

'We still have to get home first,' Michael said. He turned to Clarissa. 'What happened to you? What's the last thing you remember?'

The demons cleared their plates and brought the main course. It appeared to be roast beef with a side of traditional Western vegetables – potatoes and carrots.

'Oh, not the beef *again*,' Clarissa said with dismay.

'Apologies, ma'am,' the demon said. 'It's all we have in stock at the moment. We are expecting a new delivery soon.'

'The demons are angels looking after us,' Rhonda said as the servants left. 'But apparently their resources are very limited. There's no electricity, no refrigeration, no modern conveniences. Everything has to be brought up from – what do you call it? – the Earthly Plane.'

'It's a pain,' Clarissa said. 'Even if the King let me have a laptop, I would have nothing to plug it into.'

'So what is the last thing you remember?' Michael said.

'Laptop!' Clarissa said. 'I need to contact my parents. Do you have your phone?'

'No,' Michael said. 'They took it all away from me before they brought me up here.'

'Well damn,' she said with the amused exasperation he had always found particularly charming.

'Tell me about the last thing you remember,' he said again, beginning to wonder if she was deliberately avoiding the question.

'Oh, of course,' she said. 'We were shopping in Horizon Plaza on Ap Lei Chau, we were looking at gorgeous coffee tables made out of longhouse doors, and I went to the ladies', and they grabbed me then.'

'I remember that,' Michael said, nodding confirmation. It matched what the sentient stone in her engagement ring had said. 'They replaced you with a copy and I never knew.'

She fingered her cutlery, her expression stricken. 'That's awful. I thought you'd come and find me, I didn't know they'd replaced me. I was mad at you for a long time.'

'I know. I'm sorry. I was deceived; first I thought the copy was you, then I thought you were dead. I was misled by people I trusted.'

'What gave the copy away?'

'Some of the copies are programmed to explode.'

'Good god, that's awful,' Rhonda said. She lowered her voice. 'Michael, Clarissa and I ...' Her voice petered out. 'I mean, it's obvious that the Demon King is using us as a tool to make you do what he wants. Are you sure we're the real us?'

Michael hesitated. The Dark Lord had said that the broken and miserable Clarissa in the wheelchair back home was the real one. His mother had died, been Judged in Hell, and reattached to the wheel of rebirth. These two women had to be copies.

'But we'd know if we were copies. Surely we'd know?' Clarissa said before he could reply.

'Most of the copies were unaware,' Michael said.

'Is that why you're ...' Clarissa gestured helplessly

towards him. 'Is that why …'

He nodded silently.

'Do we look like copies?' Rhonda said.

'No,' Michael said, and she relaxed. 'But I've been fooled by copies of Clarissa before.'

Clarissa put her elbows on the table and her face in her hands. 'What if I am? What if I explode?' Her shoulders shook. 'What … what —'

'Clarissa.' Michael rose and went to her and pulled her up out of her chair and into a hug, but she pushed him away. He stood next to her without touching her and spoke intensely to her. 'It's okay. Don't worry about it for now; we'll sort it out later. I'll do this job for the King and we'll take you home and even if you are a copy, you're still my Clarissa and the Dark Lord will know what to do.'

'And if he says we're demons? And I'm a copy? And there's a real Clarissa out there, who isn't me?'

'Nothing will happen. I promise.'

'But if I'm not the real Clarissa then you'll want to be with the real one! Where will that leave me? I could be a living bomb, programmed to explode the minute I'm back home!'

'I love you.'

She looked up into his eyes, desperate, and must have seen his uncertainty because she turned and ran out. Rhonda and Michael hurried to follow her. She scurried up the stairs and along the landing, threw herself through a door and slammed it shut.

He rapped on the door. 'Clarissa?'

'Go away!' she shouted from inside.

'Michael.' Rhonda gently pushed him aside and stood next to the door. 'Clarissa? Let me in. We can talk.'

There was no reply, and Michael had a horrible vision of Clarissa harming herself in her desperation and panic.

'Clarissa, I'm in the same situation as you; I could be a copy as well. Let me in and we can talk.'

Clarissa was silent for a long moment, then she said, full of tears, 'Just you, Rhonda.'

Rhonda nodded to Michael, who nodded back.

'Go back down and finish your dinner,' Rhonda said. 'Just leave us and we'll talk tomorrow when you've rested. Find an empty guest room, there are plenty.' She opened the door gently, went inside, and closed it behind her.

Michael stood, helpless, in front of the door and didn't hear them talking. Eventually he wandered back downstairs to the dining room and sat in front of his cooling beef.

When the demons came to clear the plates, he stopped one. 'You. Wait and talk to me.'

She stopped, hovering over the plates, then stood back from the table and wrung her hands. She was in the form of a teenaged half-European, half-Chinese girl; slim and childlike, with huge, terrified eyes.

The other demons quickly took the untouched plates and returned to the kitchen, obviously pleased that they hadn't been singled out.

'What's your number?' he asked the female demon.

'I don't have one, sir,' she said, studying her hands as she twisted them together. She realised what she was doing, put her hands behind her back, and continued to look at the floor in a show of humility.

'No number? You have a name?' Michael said, surprised.

'I don't have anything, my Lord. When the masters need me they shout at me. Except for the King, who makes me do things with his will alone.'

'I understand. How long have you been here?'

She shook her head, silent.

'No idea?'

She shook her head again.

'Have you always been here?'

'I have vague memories from before I came. Nothing much, sir.'

'I won't hurt you, you can relax. I just want some answers.'

She stiffened and collapsed in on herself, bending her head even lower.

'Are there any other humans here?' he said.

'Not in this building. This building is the only one I am permitted to be in.'

'I see. Have you heard sounds that would suggest there are other people here?'

'Never, my Lord.'

He took a wild shot. 'Has the King ever discussed his plans in here?'

She went silent and dropped her head even more. She was so curled up with submission that her chin was resting on her chest.

'Thank you. Dismissed.'

Her head shot up and she gazed at him with wonder.

He waved her away. 'I mean it. Thank you, you've been very helpful. Return to your duties.'

She lit up, then quickly shut down the smile. She nodded to him and raced back into the kitchen. A minute later she returned to the dining room and bowed deeply to him. 'I thank you for your kindness, my Lord.' She slipped back into the kitchen, still full of wonder.

The demons returned with a dessert of plain sponge cake that was not only obviously pre-packed, it had seen better days – it was dry and crumbly. The serving demon – a different one – cringed away from him as she placed the plate in front of him.

'Don't worry, I won't hurt you,' he said to her, and she jumped. She didn't reply, she just ran into the kitchen.

He fiddled with the cake for a while then rose and left the dining room. He checked Clarissa's door; no sound from behind it. He rapped on it and was ignored. He sent his senses inside; both women were in there, asleep. Rhonda had obviously nodded off sitting on the bed with Clarissa's head in her lap. He smiled slightly at the fond relationship they had developed, and wished for a moment that this was real and they could come home with him and be a loving family. He shook his head; that was for later. Right now he had a job to do.

He went down the stairs to the entry hall and tried the front door but it was securely locked even though there was no locking mechanism he could see. He could use his metal abilities to dismantle it but it felt like vandalism to destroy something so beautiful. He wandered through the ground floor until he found the kitchen; the work surfaces were stainless steel but the stove was a huge wood-fired one and there was no refrigerator. The demons were busy washing the plates and all stopped when he entered.

'Where are the deliveries brought in?' he asked them.

One of the quivering demons pointed at the solid metal kitchen door. He tried it and it was locked in the same way as the front door.

'Can anyone open it? I want to go for a walk and get some fresh air,' he said.

The demons all shook their heads. The same slim girl was pushed forward by her comrades to speak to him. 'They open the door when there is a delivery, my Lord,' she said.

'I see. Thank you,' he said.

He put his hand on the door handle, gave it a

good tug with his full strength, and it didn't open. He softened the metal slightly and felt it sag beneath his touch. He spun it back together, then went back out to the entry hall. He'd go out exploring later when the demons were shut down for the night.

The other rooms on the ground floor were furnished with European-style pieces that were detailed with inlays of wood and semi-precious stones without being overly ornate. There was a large, comfortable living room with many cushions on the floor, still appearing as new, and a massive black glass fireplace that would be a feature of the room on a cold night. He looked up; the construction was silver amalgam and glass panels, and he wondered how the ceiling–floor interface worked.

The next room was a library, holding old-fashioned leather-bound volumes. He took one down and opened it to find hand-written and brilliantly decorated text. The subject matter was obvious; detailed techniques for forging high-quality steel, complete with diagrams and instructions. He closed the book and looked around. The room was filled with these priceless manuscripts. One of these books may contain the secrets of creating the buildings and lowering the gravity. His memorisation skills were non-existent and he wouldn't be able to carry the library away with him, so he would have to find a way to return and collect them after he'd left.

He went up the stairs and along the balcony that circled the entry hall. Each door led into a guest room and they all appeared identical. The one next to Clarissa's had obviously been lived in for a while; his mother's room. He went into the room next to that and sat on the bed. Each room had a bath and washbasin in a corner but no separation from the sleeping and washing parts, except that the glass-tiled floor around the bed was covered in finely woven rugs depicting pine branches. A heavy wardrobe stood next to the wall and he opened it; it was full of the soft cotton unisex robes that Clarissa and Rhonda were wearing, all in pastel shades of blue and grey. A chest of drawers held female underwear and cotton breeches. Another guest room would probably hold clothing for a man and he went out to find one.

He found male clothes in the next room, robes and breeches that would fit him, and male underwear. He fell onto the bed and looked at the ceiling. The time difference between Western China and Northern Europe must have been ridiculous and it was probably insanely early in the morning where he was from, but he wasn't tired at all – he was too overwrought at the thought of these wonderful women who were intelligent and self-aware, who considered themselves his mother and fiancée, and who were demon copies.

He woke later with a start. He had a moment of disorientation before he realised where he was. The room's window was dark and he had no idea how long he'd slept. He pulled himself out of bed feeling gritty and needing a shower, but he didn't know how long he had until dawn, when his captors would come for him.

Teleportation out of the mansion was impossible – his teleportation skills were blocked again. Time to do it the old-fashioned way. He went as silently as he could out of his room onto the darkened landing; all the other doors were closed. He sent his senses out; Rhonda and Clarissa were both still asleep in Clarissa's room and he didn't disturb them. He went downstairs and opened the door to the kitchen to find all the demons lying on the floor or sitting against the wall. No way could he creep through there without waking them. He returned to the entry and had an inspiration; he flew up to the ceiling to take a glass panel out and go exploring.

He flew too high and hard in the low gravity and crashed into the glass. He stopped and hovered just below it. He heard movement; someone had heard the noise and was waiting to see if it occurred again before investigating. After a few minutes of silent hovering he put his hand on the glass panel and unravelled the metal holding it. The panel fell into his hands and was liftable – heavy, but liftable – and he flew through the opening it made in the ceiling and placed it on the roof to one side.

The sky was mostly dark with a brighter smudge on the eastern horizon – dawn soon. The air was bracingly cold and full of the suggestion of snow. He tried to teleport again and failed; something about the nature of these European Heavens was severely limiting his powers.

He flew higher over the city and sent his senses out. There were life signatures of birds and small animals, but nothing larger than a rat. He flew a kilometre over the breathtaking spires and found a building that looked promising; six storeys high, and more blunt and utilitarian than the prevailing airy decorative style. He landed in front of its door and tried it, and it swung open easily.

It was another library, with a vast central atrium the full six storeys tall and stacks of shelving containing hand-lettered and bound manuscripts, covered in a light layer of dust. The floor hadn't been walked on in a very long time. The amount of knowledge held there was awe-inspiring. Due to the Celestial nature of the location, he had no trouble reading the shelf labels: there were books on history, philosophy, engineering and 'magic'. He opened a magic book and it was detailed descriptions of something identical to the Asian methods of energy manipulation – chi gong and martial arts. He walked up a flight of spiral stairs to the first level: medicine and history. He opened a history book and it contained a detailed description of the Roman expansion two thousand years before. He shook his head as he returned the book to the shelf; he had to find a way to retrieve this treasure from the demons' control.

Something shifted in the corner of his eye and he turned. The building was changing – the metal brightened from grey to almost white and the dust disappeared. He watched with wonder as the structure around him flared into life, the crystalline lamps becoming more brilliant and the glass clearer and more perfect.

A rhythmic banging began some distance away and it took him a moment to realise that it was the sound of a helicopter. He sent his senses out: it was the Demon King, returning with a Shen whose nature was completely different from any Michael had experienced before – the spirit of the city. The city must be responding to its spirit's return.

The Demon King needed to stay unaware of his ability to leave the mansion otherwise he would probably be locked up. He rushed out the door of the library, closed it behind him, and flew as quickly as he could back to the mansion with sound of the helicopter's rotors seeming directly behind him. He flew through the roof and replaced the panel with a quick weld of the amalgam. He hoped that was enough to hold it as he flew down to the bedroom he'd chosen.

His feet touched the landing just as the front door opened and the King entered with the spirit of the city.

'Prince Michael,' the King said, moving forward to speak to him. 'Please come down here.'

Michael took a huge stride over the balcony balustrade and landed in front of the King on the floor below. He studied the spirit of the city; it appeared as an elderly European man in a brown robe similar to a monk's habit. The hood was thrown back and the man had long grey hair held in a braid that fell down his back and a long beard fastened in multiple smaller braids. His intelligent green eyes studied Michael curiously.

'How did you get out of the mansion?' the King said, his voice sharp with controlled anger.

Michael considered playing dumb for a moment and decided it wasn't worth the effort. 'The building's made of metal.'

'And?'

'And I'm my father's son. I could dismantle the entire building in less than five minutes.'

The King turned back to speak to the spirit. 'Is there a building in this city that isn't made of metal?'

The spirit smiled slightly, and when he spoke his voice was warm and rich. 'No. I'm one hundred per cent silver, except for the parts that are glass.'

The King turned back to Michael and concentrated for a moment. Five huddling, terrified demons came out of the kitchen.

'Go up and get the young one and bring her down here,' the King ordered without looking at them.

'No, wait. Why do you want her?' Michael said.

'No bamboo here, I'll have to stick slivers of wood under her fingernails.'

Michael reeled back, nauseous. 'Don't hurt her! Why would you want to do that?'

The demons stopped halfway up the stairs.

'Will you vow to remain in this building?' the King said.

'I give you my word,' Michael said. 'I won't leave the building. There's no need to hurt either of them!'

The King waved the demon servants away, again without looking at them. 'Good.' He gestured behind him towards the spirit of the city. 'Semias, this is Michael. Michael's visiting from the Asian Heavens, he's the son of the spirit of their western heavens. I want you take him to see the gravity engine.'

'He just vowed never to leave the building,' Semias said.

The King gestured with frustration. 'He can leave it to go to the engine!'

'Very well,' Semias said. 'Michael, was it? Come with me.' He held his thin, pale hand out to Michael.

Michael took his hand and heard the Demon King say, 'Wait, what?' as the mansion disappeared.

The room around them changed to a vast hall, fifty metres high and three times that long, nearly filled by an enormous shining brass cube. Michael's mouth fell open; they were standing on a walkway halfway up the building that circled the hall and gave a good view of the cube. Lights sparkled and sank around the structure, and the glass-tiled floor around it rippled in expanding circles. He sent his sense out to check where they were and found himself deep underground. No tunnels led into the room; it was only reachable by teleportation.

He jerked back as Semias moved right up into his face to challenge him, the spirit's expression rigid with anger.

'What the hell is going on here, young man?' the spirit said. 'Why are there Asian demons here, what are those two poor women doing here, and more than anything what the hell are *you* doing here?'

Michael opened and closed his mouth a few times then pulled himself together. 'I was hoping you could tell me that. Why are you working with them?'

'I'm not. They're forcing me to cooperate.' The spirit sagged and turned to face the machine, leaning on the railing. 'I need answers.'

Michael leaned on the railing next to him. 'So do I, sir.'

'How did you travel up here? Our world is

blocked off and nobody should be able to enter.'

'The Asian Demon King brought me. I have no idea how he did it. The gateway was a cathedral in Rotterdam.'

Semias banged his hand on the brass railing. 'This should not have happened!' He turned to Michael and jabbed a finger in his face. 'If you're the son of one of the Asian spirits, you shouldn't be working with him.'

'I'm not. I came to investigate, and discovered that he's holding my mother and fiancée.'

'And he threatened to torture them if you don't cooperate.' Semias sagged and leaned back on the railing. 'Do you know what he wants?'

'Mostly he wants control of the Asian Heavens. It looks like he's already invaded the European ones. Why didn't the Shen here stop him?'

'Shen?'

'God? Spirits?' Michael shook his head. 'It's what we call ourselves in Asia.'

'Calling them Sidhe would be close enough. They're gone. It's just me here, guarding the empty Heavens.'

'So why didn't *you* stop them? They're demons and they should not be here!'

'You think I didn't try?' Semias said, his voice fierce with anger. 'I have no idea how they made it up here. When they came to my city I blocked them, I closed my gates and made my walls slippery and unclimbable – and that bastard took a huge mechanical *battering ram* to me. He broke the glass and framework on my eastern gates …' He dropped his head and shook it. 'Do you have any idea much it hurts if I'm dismantled without any preparation or proper care? It was agony. Torture. I fought them, but they broke into me.' He raised his head and glared at Michael again. 'And when you took a piece out of the palace's ceiling it gave me a massive headache.'

'Sorry,' Michael said. 'But we need to find a way to stop them. How many demons are here in the European Heavens? Are there more than a hundred?'

'Three thousand.'

'Holy *shit*.'

'But that's just the big ones. There are six thousand small ones as well.'

Michael was speechless.

'You're a Sidhe yourself, I can see it. Kill yourself now and go home and warn them. Tell them what's happening here.'

Michael gestured towards the cube. 'What if the demons work out the secret of the gravity?'

'We're underground, a hundred feet below the city, and nobody but me can travel here. There's no other way in. Go now while they're waiting for us to return.'

'I can't leave my mother and fiancée. I have to take them back with me.'

'They're demons, lad. Leave them.'

'Are you sure?'

Semias hesitated.

Michael turned away. 'Yeah. Neither am I.'

'It's hard to tell,' Semias said. 'Your fiancée isn't from my region, and your mother has an unusual part-demonic nature. She may be a descendent of the ancient Serpent people.'

'What Serpent people? I've heard that before. Tell me about them, I think it's important.'

'We don't have time. The Demon King just pulled your fiancée down to the entrance hall and is threatening her if we don't return immediately. We need to go.'

Semias teleported them back to find the Demon King in the mansion's foyer, yelling at a terrified Clarissa, who was being held by two guards. When he saw Semias and Michael he rounded on them. 'Next time do what I tell you!'

'I did exactly what you told me to, I took him to see the engine,' Semias said.

Michael ran to Clarissa and pulled her out of the demon guards' grasps. 'Did he hurt you?' He held her close and brushed his hand over her hair. 'Are you all right?'

'I didn't touch her. She broke down herself, the coward,' the Demon King said.

'Leave her alone!' Michael pulled back to see her face, and his heart broke when it mirrored the haunted Clarissa back at the Western Palace. 'Clarissa, honey? Talk to me.'

'Where's Rhonda?' Clarissa clutched him. 'Can I go back to my room? I want to be away from here.'

Semias disappeared, then reappeared with Rhonda. She ran to Clarissa and Michael released his fiancée into his mother's arms. Rhonda led Clarissa, still dazed, up the stairs to their rooms.

'Next time don't take anyone anywhere without my permission or I'll put you back in your cell,' the Demon King said to Semias with venom. He turned to Michael. 'Did you see the gravity engine?'

'Yes.'

'What does it look like?'

Michael hesitated. 'You won't believe me.'

'Try me.'

'It's a brass cube. Featureless. No external moving parts.'

The King nodded, unsurprised. 'All right. Now both of you listen carefully to me. Michael, if you can map the internal workings of the engine and provide me with a blueprint, I'll let you and the women go back to the Asian Heavens, free and unharmed. Semias.'

'I know,' Semias said. 'If I give him the information

you'll leave me here in the city and I won't be kept
locked up and separated from myself any more.'

'That's the deal. Will you both cooperate?'

'I will,' Michael said.

'Very well, I will as well,' Semias said. 'Let the
boy eat and rest, he's falling over on his feet. I'll take
him back this afternoon and we'll map out the internal
structure for you.'

'Provide me with an incorrect blueprint and I will
knock every tower in this city down, one by one.' The
Demon King glared at Michael. 'And if I don't produce
a working identical engine from the blueprint you give
me, I will hunt down everybody you love and I will
torture them to death myself.'

Michael slept through most of the day and went out to
the dining room as dusk was falling, feeling dehydrated
and exhausted. Neither of the women were there, and
he went up to their rooms and rapped on their doors.
He sent his senses into the room, searching for them,
and didn't find them. They weren't anywhere in the
building. He stormed back down to the kitchen and
yelled at the cowering demons.

'Where are Rhonda and Clarissa?'

'The King took them, my Lord,' the small female
demon said. 'He said to pass on the message that he will
hold them safe until you produce what he wants.'

'Where's Semias?'

'Who?'

Semias appeared next to him. 'I'm all around
you, lad, I am the city. Eat something …' He looked
around. 'Not good enough.' He concentrated, and the
kitchen glowed into life. Preserved meat, smoked and
netted, hung from the hooks on the sides of the walls,
and baskets of vegetables appeared next to the stove.
'Feed the boy and then we'll get to work.'

He led Michael into the dining room, which gleamed with even more splendour while the spirit was present, and sat him at the table.

'Can we do this?' Michael said.

'We can,' Semias said, sitting next to him. 'Do you think they'll keep their side of the bargain?'

'There's a small chance they will,' Michael said.

'Can you find the women and teleport to them? Take them out now and leave.'

'I don't know where they are. Do you?'

'They're not within the city.'

Michael rubbed his hands over his face with defeat. 'I don't have any choice. I have to help him. I just hope he doesn't find too many military uses for the technology when we unlock it for him.'

'Don't worry, he won't.'

The demons emerged from the kitchen with plates of food. Suddenly Michael was starving and Semias remained silent as Michael wolfed the meal down.

After he'd eaten they returned to the gravity engine room and stood on the walkway. Michael turned his metal senses into it and stood for a moment, bewildered, as he watched it work. It appeared to be clockwork; cogs and springs worked in jerky mechanical motion within it, but there were places inside the engine where the mechanics didn't mesh. It was like looking at the interior of a clock through a shattered window.

'What the hell is going on in there?' he said.

'You can see inside?' Semias said.

Michael nodded a reply, moving along the walkway to get a view from a different angle. Some of the pieces appeared to be only half a cog, but still turning as if they were circular. The nature of the interior was giving him a headache.

'It's four dimensional,' Semias said. 'All of the movement is in three dimensions, but it's bent through four. That's where the weird interior joins are.'

'I see,' Michael said. 'The Sidhe could work in four dimensions?'

'Can you teleport, lad?'

'No,' Michael said, confused at the sudden change of topic. 'I'm stuck here. Something about this place screws my head up.' He rubbed the back of his skull, which was still tender. 'Or there's permanent brain damage from being smacked around too much in the last week or so. Wouldn't be the first time.'

'Could you teleport before you arrived here, though?'

'Well, yeah.'

'That's moving in four dimensions. You lift yourself above the flat piece of paper that is our reality, and drop yourself somewhere else, moving through the fourth dimension. You do it yourself.'

'But …' Michael shook his head. 'Okay, if you say so, all this advanced physics is beyond me. But I can't manipulate things like the interior of that machine.'

'No, I do that. I have multi-dimensional control within my city. All the parts were built by our artisans, and then I put it together.'

'I see.' Michael turned back to the engine and leaned on the railing. 'Will you build it for them?'

'Until they release you I don't think I have a choice,' Semias said, his voice low. He straightened and became more brisk. 'Now, we have to find a way to very accurately measure the components while they're moving, because it is important that they all be made in exactly the same ratio.'

'Ratio? What about the size of the whole machine? Isn't that important?'

'Oh, the size of the whole engine is completely vital. The smaller it is, the more gravity it negates. An engine a foot to a side will send a large chunk of the planet shooting out into space and bouncing away from every gravity well it encounters.'

Michael leaned on the rail and considered for a moment.

'Yes,' Semias said.

Michael turned to him. 'What?'

'Yes. We'll tell them that they can make it small and portable, then ensure that you and the women are safe when they turn it on. The demon leader will be gone forever, and me with him.'

Michael turned back to the machine. 'I'd prefer not to sacrifice you, Semias. You've cared for my family and been honourable in your assistance.'

'As long as the city stands, I exist,' Semias said. 'I don't breathe or eat.' He raised his head and spoke contemplatively. 'I wouldn't mind going out and visiting the stars, seeing if there's any intelligences out there like me. Once the demons are destroyed I can turn the machine on and off to control where I go.' He turned to Michael and smiled. 'It would be an interesting experience. So.' He banged the rail with his palm. 'Let's build the blueprint and see where this little adventure takes us.'

It was very late when they returned to the mansion. Michael checked for the women and they hadn't returned; he was alone. He went into the room he'd commandeered and washed, then put on some of the soft cotton boxers from the chest of drawers and fell onto the bed. He pulled the covers over him, and their lavender scent soothed him. He was asleep before he knew it.

He woke and sat up. The windows were bright and it felt like he'd slept a long time. He turned and saw someone kneeling on the floor next to the bed. It was one of the demons; a young female, but different to the one he'd spoken to before.

'Get out,' he said.

'I have a message for you,' she said. She bowed low over her knees. 'Please do not destroy me, Highness, I only bear a message.'

'Who from?'

'The Number One Son of the Demon King.'

'Wait outside for me for a moment. I need to dress,' he said.

'I will sit here and not look, Highness.'

'I need to use the bathroom as well!' he said, exasperated. 'Wait outside.'

'The bathroom?' She looked around, then her eyes widened. 'Oh, I most sincerely apologise. I will wait.' She climbed to her feet, bowed to him, and crept out.

He opened the door when he was done and she was standing next to it. He checked around; nobody else present except for the demons in the kitchen. He gestured for her to enter.

She came into the centre of the room and knelt again. 'Royal Highness.'

'What's the message?'

She stiffened as if she'd been struck, then relaxed and her whole body language changed. She became graceful and confident as she pulled herself to her feet, then sauntered to the arm chair at the side of the room and lounged in it. She waved one hand. 'Good to see you again, Prince Michael. Please, take a seat, let's talk.'

Michael sat on the bed and waited.

'The King's selling us out to them,' the female demon said. 'He's promised the horde that he'll take the Earthly back and we'll walk in the sun again. He's promised that when he's taken the Earthly he'll march on the Heavens themselves.' She leaned forward and put her elbows on her knees. 'But even if he succeeds, it will be with the help of the European Demon King, and the debt will need to be paid in the end, and the debt will mean the enslavement of us all.' She leaned back. 'I can't let that happen. I'd rather we stayed in Hell than became the thralls of the European King. We need to stop him. We can help each other. What is he asking you to do, and why are you helping him?'

'He has my mother and my fiancée,' Michael said.

'Are you sure they're not copies? Your mother died when she took the Elixir of Immortality. And I'm pretty sure your fiancée was experimented on and tortured until the Dark Lord rescued her.'

Michael looked down at his hands and didn't reply.

'You won't risk the chance that they're real?' the demon said.

Michael shook his head.

'I understand. Well, I don't really understand, your Celestial minds are beyond me, but I'm willing to work around it. Why is the King holding you? Are you a hostage against your father?'

'He needs my abilities with metal.'

'Oh,' the demon said, a drawn-out sound of understanding. 'The gravity engine.'

Semias appeared at the end of the bed. 'Who is this?'

'This is the Number One Son of the Demon King,' Michael said. 'He's possessing this servant to speak to me.'

'Do your demons work the way ours do?' Semias said. 'Is he plotting against his father to take the throne?'

'Always,' the demon said.

'I see,' Semias said. 'Can we speak freely here? I'm sure the Demon King has spies listening to us.'

'As long as I'm here they can't hear anything,' the demon said. 'Talk to me.'

A chair appeared and Semias sat in it. 'So what's in it for us?'

'I don't want him to succeed, he's working with the European demons —' the demon began.

'I know all this, I heard everything you said,' Semias said. 'I'll ask the question again. What's in it for us?'

'If I can free the women and return them to your care, what will you do?' the demon said.

'I'd leave immediately but I can't teleport out,' Michael said.

'I can open a gateway for you,' Semias said.

'Then I'll leave,' Michael said. 'Take them and go.'

'Promise?'

'My word.'

'All right.' The demon rose. 'Let me see if I can find them, and we can stop this before it starts.' The demon's face went slack, and then filled with comprehension. She bowed low to Michael. 'Highness. Please permit me to return to the kitchen.'

Michael waved her away. 'Go.'

She bowed again and went out.

'Have something to eat and we'll return to the engine,' Semias said.

Five days later, Michael and Semias returned to the mansion with the rolled-up plans. Michael went into the dining room and opened the kitchen door to speak to the demons.

'Tell the King we're finished.'

The demons, who had frozen when they saw him, nodded. He went back into the dining room, tossed the plans onto the table and sat. He put his head in his hands and waited.

'It'll be fine, lad,' Semias said. 'He'll give you your family back.'

Michael nodded into his hands without replying.

Two hours later the noise of the Demon King's helicopter woke him and he raised his head from the table. He waited quietly as the King approached and entered the mansion. When the King came into the dining room, Michael pushed the plans towards him.

'My side of the bargain. Now let my mother and fiancée go.'

The King rolled the blueprints open and studied them. He glanced up at Michael and Semias. 'What the fuck is this? This is a bunch of oddly shaped pieces that won't fit together into any sort of cube.'

'It's the best we could do considering the four-dimensional nature of the mechanism,' Michael said. 'If you build these pieces, Semias can put it together.'

'What are these cogs made of? What metal?'

'A very specific brass alloy, which will be almost impossible to smelt ...' Michael's voice petered out, and he put his head in his hands again. He was too exhausted to think straight.

'Oh, Michael,' Semias said with compassion.

The King looked down at the plans, studying them, then back up at Michael. He pushed the paper at him. 'You have metal abilities. Make it for us.'

Michael slammed his hands on the table. 'You said you'd let us go!'

'You just said yourself that you're the only one who can make it.'

'Bring the women back.'

'When it's built and working, I won't just bring them back, I'll drop all three of you in the most expensive suite in the Beijing Four Seasons.'

Michael didn't have the energy to fight him. 'I

need a hundred kilos of copper, forty-five kilos of zinc, and ten kilos each of iron and tin.'

'That's not enough metal to make the huge machine down there.'

'Size doesn't matter,' Michael said. 'Smaller will be easier to make.'

The King looked sharply from Michael to Semias. 'If size doesn't matter then why is the one down there so fucking huge?'

'How do you know how big it is?' Michael said.

'Fibre optic cameras on the end of a drill,' the King said.

'What's that?' Semias said.

'It means that they can stick a pole into the earth and see what's at the end. They know how big it is.'

'So why is that one so big and this one so small?' the King said, tapping the plans with his finger.

'Aesthetics,' Semias said.

The King's mouth fell open. 'What?'

'Bigger is more inspiring.'

'That makes no sense at all. You wasted resources to make it *pretty*?'

'Making things pretty is the *whole point*,' Semias said.

The King hesitated, glaring at him, then said, 'I suppose it is.' He straightened. 'You tigers can change one metal to another. What if I gave you a hundred kilos of scrap?'

'It will double the time I take to synthesise the machine,' Michael said.

'I can wait.' The King hesitated. 'Hold on, how long to make it?'

'With the right raw materials, three days. With scrap, double it.'

'You can't do it that quickly, lad,' Semias said.

'If it means getting my family out of here, I'll

work day and night on it,' Michael said.

'All right.' The King nodded. 'Well done. I'll have the metal for you within forty-eight hours.'

'I want to see my family.'

'As soon as this is made, Prince Michael, they are yours.'

'Let me speak to them before I start to build anything.'

'I'll see what I can do,' the King said. 'Rest and eat while I gather the materials for you. Believe me, I would let you go now, but I want this to work and you're the best way of ensuring it. Humour me and build it.'

'I just want Rhonda and Clarissa free and unharmed,' Michael said.

'Then we both want the same thing. I'll be back with the metal.' He turned and left.

Semias sat at the table across from Michael. 'Any word?'

Michael shook his head.

'Do as the King said. You've been working yourself into the ground. I think you've had about two hours' sleep every night. Rest and eat until he brings you the metal.'

Michael rubbed his gritty eyes. 'I just want to go home with my family.'

'We'll get you there, lad. It will happen.'

Michael didn't reply. He should have been on the way home with the women he loved, but he wasn't surprised at having to stay and build the damn thing.

Three days later he was going nearly mad with inactivity, even though he and Semias were evenly matched at chess, when the helicopter thundered overhead. He went to the entry and waited, watching with his Inner Eye as the demons unloaded a crate full of the metal that he required. He wished his Eye could do more damage as the King approached and opened the door.

'Do you mind? That's extremely uncomfortable,' the King said as he came in.

Michael closed his Inner Eye.

'Thank you,' the King said. 'I have the metal, and it's the right elements as well. You said three days?'

'I want to speak to my family first. Let me talk to my mother and fiancée and I'll get right to work.'

'I thought you might say that,' the King said. He gestured with his head towards the living room. 'In here.'

Michael followed the King into the room and watched, standing, as the King pulled a tablet computer out of his laptop bag and flipped it up onto its stand. He placed it on a side table and indicated for Michael to join him.

'We had to set up our own communication network, the logistics were a nightmare,' the King said as he turned the tablet on. 'But we have it working.' He leaned back. 'There you are.'

Rhonda and Clarissa appeared on the screen, obviously in front of a webcam. Michael gasped; Clarissa appeared fine but Rhonda looked terrible. She'd lost weight, her eyes were sunken and had blackened rings around them, and her skin hung from her emaciated face.

Michael rounded on the King. 'What did you do to her?'

'Nothing,' the King said, raising his hands. 'Being here in the Heavens isn't good for her, probably because of her part-demon nature. She can't survive here much longer, Prince Michael, you need to finish the engine so I can release her.'

Michael turned back to the screen. Rhonda looked terrible, but Clarissa looked okay? Maybe Rhonda was a copy and Clarissa was the original … He couldn't risk it.

'Mom? How are you holding up? You look unwell.'

'I'm fine, really,' Rhonda said with forced cheerfulness. 'They're looking after me but they say something about my nature doesn't suit these Heavens.' She leaned into the screen. 'The King says you can take us home in three days?'

Michael touched the screen, wishing he could comfort them directly. 'Three days and we're out of here. I'll take you home. I promise.'

'We trust you,' Clarissa said, and clutched Rhonda's hand. 'I always knew you would protect me, Michael. You'll find us a way out of this.'

'I will.'

'All right, that's enough,' the King said. He turned the tablet off and folded it up. 'If you hurry on this you can have them home with you in three days. I promise as well.'

'My mother may not last three days!' Michael said.

'She's fine. I've seen others like this – it takes them years to fade. Really. You just need to pull her out of the Heavens and get her back on the Earthly where she belongs. Will you start work on the engine for me?'

'Show me where the metal is,' Michael said.

'Right this way.'


When night fell, Michael moved the metal into the entry hall of the palace where it was warmer. Producing the cogs was fiddly and time-consuming, but once he had a few cast in the right shape his work sped up. It was deep into the night when one of the demons entered, left him a cup of something, and left again. He tasted it; some sort of warm grape juice, sweetened with honey. He drank it without really noticing as he worked on the gears, making sure that they fitted together perfectly.

He stopped to take a sip of the drink and something hit his mouth. Revolted, he peered into the cup and saw a packet in the bottom. He looked around; nobody nearby. He took the drink with him up to his room, ostensibly to use the bathroom, and when he was inside he quickly untied the oilskin packet and read the message scribbled on it.

*Three hundred kilometres north-north-west of you, in a large rectangular mansion on the coast between England and Wales. Follow coastline where the two regions join and you will find it easily.*

He didn't even need to do that; when he was fifty kilometres from them he'd be able to sense them. He raised his head. 'Semias.'

Semias appeared next to him. 'I know. We need to go down into the engine room again, and compare the work we've done with what's in place there.'

Michael put his hand out, Semias took it, and they teleported into the engine room where they could talk freely.

'I know that place,' Semias said. 'There's a large island off the west coast, and this estate is where the channel is at its narrowest. It's surrounded by lawns and gardens. It'll be a cleared area in the middle of a large forest; you can't miss it.'

'It's a long way away, can you carry me there?' Michael said.

'No. Best I can do is the edge of the city. Can you do the rest of the way?'

'Of course.' Michael put his hand out and Semias took it again. They landed on the glass wall that surrounded the city.

Michael slapped Semias on the shoulder. 'I will be back for you.'

'You can't take a whole city with you, lad,' Semias

said. 'Just go and leave me to it. Free your family.'

'I won't forget what you've done for me,' Michael said. 'We will return and clear the demons from the European Heavens.'

'Just go!' Semias said with urgency. 'They could return any time.'

Michael clasped Semias's hand then released it and flew up and west.

He kept flying west, though the cold night sky of the deserted Heavens. The Asian Heavens were full of the telepathic buzz and energy signatures of the Shen that lived there; these skies were eerily silent. The cold and emptiness bit into him, and he missed the warmth and camaraderie of his brothers and sisters back in the White Tiger's palace. The skies blazed with stars overhead and he was glad for his ability to see in the dark.

It was obvious when he approached the estate where his family were being held – it registered as a seething mass of demonkind. He approached the manor carefully and felt the women's presence inside, on the top floor. Stupid demons, that was the easiest place to free them. Unless it was a trap for him, but he couldn't see any reason for them to suspect he knew where the women were.

The manor was as Semias had described – about a hundred metres long, three storeys high, with a tall ground floor that was double the height of the others. The land around it had been cleared and planted with a variety of domestic flowers, the gardens overgrown and tangled from neglect.

He landed silently on the roof and sent his senses down through it. Rhonda and Clarissa were in the room directly below him, playing cards at a table in a bedroom they obviously shared. Demons filled every other room, all the way through the mansion, and some of the demons were enormous. His best bet was to sneak in the window, grab the women, and run back to Semias's city where the spirit could open the gateway to Rotterdam for them. He made himself invisible and floated down to hover outside their window.

*Mom,* he said. *Don't say anything, but I'm just outside the window. I'm here to get you out.*

Rhonda looked up and nodded.

*There are demons everywhere. All around you. Just a sec, I'll tell Clarissa.* He changed to Clarissa. *Hello, my darling, I'm here to get you. I just spoke to Mom. Don't say anything but I'm floating outside the window. Nod if you understand.*

Both women were nodding now, smiling conspiratorially. Clarissa shivered with delight.

*Careful,* he said. *They're watching you. Can you open the window, Mom?*

Rhonda shook her head.

*Okay. Can both of you move closer to it?*

Clarissa and Rhonda put their cards down, wandered to the window and made a show of looking out.

'It's so beautiful here,' Clarissa said. 'I wish they'd let us out to go for a walk or something. Anything.'

'I know. It's awful being cooped up,' Rhonda said.

*Both of you get Best Actress trophies when we're home,* Michael said, and the women shared another grin. *That's too close, I'm going to break it. Either side against the wall, on three.*

He counted to three, the women moved, and he burst through the window and landed in the middle of the room amid a shower of glass. He took a few seconds to heal the cuts – he didn't need to be losing blood while they were on the run – then scooped the women up, one on each arm, and jumped out the window again.

He'd grabbed them clumsily and both were in danger of slipping out of his grasp, so he flew as fast as he could for a hundred metres then landed.

'Just need to get a better grip on you,' he said, releasing them to shift his hold. There was a loud bang, something smacked him on the shoulder and he reeled forward. The demons had shot him. He grabbed Clarissa with his left arm but his right wouldn't move – his shoulder joint was shattered and his right arm hung uselessly, the fabric of his robe torn and bloody. He didn't have time to heal something that big; it could take hours. He blocked the nerve endings before the pain really hit and tried to ignore it.

'Leave me and take Clarissa,' Rhonda said. 'I'm a copy.'

'No, I'm taking you both,' Michael said. 'Clarissa, on my back. Mom, in my left arm. I can do it.'

He turned so that Clarissa could climb onto his back and stopped. The demon with the gun was standing three metres away, pointing it at them. At least twenty other demons, some also with firearms, stood behind it. He checked the other way and it was clear.

*Quick, hop on*, he said to Clarissa, but she didn't move, frozen with terror at the gun pointed at her head.

This was the same as when he'd been in the nest and his brothers had been shot, and he knew what he had to do. He'd had weeks to think about what he should have done: in the nest, he hadn't had the common sense to open his Inner Eye on the demons and destroy the lot before they could hurt anybody. Well, now he did. He pushed the women behind him, then raised his left hand in surrender.

'We'll come quietly,' he said. 'Don't hurt them.'

The demon lowered the weapon slightly and he did it. He opened his Inner Eye on them and they all shredded in the blast of the unshielded vision of his Immortal soul. None of them was big enough to resist it. All gone.

'Okay,' he said, smiling. He turned back to Clarissa and Rhonda. 'Quickly, before more come. Let's go.'

He had a horrified moment of realisation as he looked straight into Rhonda's disbelieving face, then she and Clarissa were destroyed as well. He closed his Eye but it was too late. They were gone.

He fell to his knees on the grass, too shocked to think. He needed to go back and do that again, and this time close his Inner Eye. He hadn't done that. It didn't happen. He put his head in his hands. They were demon copies anyway – but what did that matter when they thought they were real? He'd destroyed them with a *look*. He was a monster. He wanted to kill himself. So stupid. Couldn't he go back and do that again? He felt a rush of nausea, and wanted to curl up into a ball and die. Well, good luck with that one, Mister Immortal, no dying for you.

He heard the sound of their feet approaching.

'He seems incapacitated. Let's take him back to the King,' one of the demons said.

'Fuck you,' Michael said, and blew his brains out with a blast of his own Shen energy.

He landed in Court Ten in front of Judge Clear Skies Pao the Incorruptible. He sagged with relief and grief; he was home. He knelt in front of the judge high above him on the dais and bowed his head, wiping his eyes.

'Where have you been?' Judge Pao said.

'I've been in the European Heavens failing my duty and my allegiance,' Michael said. 'Don't be lenient on me.'

Pao rose from his desk. 'I will judge the prisoner

in my private rooms. Bring him.' He stomped down the stairs off the dais and the guards grabbed Michael by the arms and pulled him to his feet to follow. They led Michael up the stairs to the judge's private quarters, dropped him on the rug in front of Pao's desk, and waited.

'Dismissed,' Pao said, sitting behind the desk.

The guards went out. Michael bent over his knees, feeling that his centre had been torn from his body. He was empty.

'Where were you, lad?' Pao said.

'In the European Heavens,' Michael said. 'Failing the Celestial. You know that.'

'The European Heavens are outside my jurisdiction,' Pao said. 'Tell me everything that happened. No, wait.' He raised one hand and his eyes unfocussed. 'Present yourself to Minor Hearing Room Four immediately. The Celestial will question you himself.' Pao rapped the desk. 'The Jade Emperor wants to talk to you, boy. Move.'

Michael rubbed his hands over his face and teleported to the Celestial Palace. The gigantic main gates had a small door at the base that opened to let him through. When he was inside the compound he took a step forward. 'Hearing Room Four.'

He walked into a small, high-walled courtyard with an ornamental bonsai tree on a carved rock in its centre. He stepped up on to the wooden veranda, then entered the small hearing room. The Jade Emperor and his father, the White Tiger of the West, were both present, and he fell to his knees in front of them and chanted the Imperial Obeisance.

The Jade Emperor waved him forward. 'Come and sit with us and tell us all you learnt.'

Michael rose and sat on the third couch, across from the two Emperors. 'I've been there for two weeks and learned next to nothing.'

'Tell us all,' the Jade Emperor said.

Michael put it together in his head, then gave them a short summary without mentioning Rhonda and Clarissa. He told them about the city, the gravity engine and Semias.

'So where are the blueprints to the gravity engine?' the Tiger said. 'That could be extremely useful.'

'I left them behind,' Michael said.

'How could you leave them behind? You spent two weeks drawing them up and left them there?'

Michael nodded silently.

'You were in their libraries and saw all their gathered wisdom and brought back none of it?' the Jade Emperor said.

'I learned that the Shen are all gone and the demons have invaded the European Heavens,' Michael said.

'We knew that already,' the Tiger said. 'The Dark Lord has been there for two days and learned more than you did in two weeks. He knows about the demons and Shen and he's looking for a way in as well. I sent Three and Four to Rotterdam, but the entrance through the cathedral is closed.'

Michael remained silent.

The Tiger threw himself back on the sofa. 'What a fucking waste of time.' He nodded to the Jade Emperor. 'Apologies.' He turned back to Michael. 'Two weeks there and you gained us *nothing*. Why the hell didn't you come home and report the minute you knew the way in? Why did you hang around there and fucking *help* them with this gravity engine and then *forget* it? You should have come back down straight away and showed us how to break in! Dammit, Number One.' He sighed loudly. 'I should demote you.'

'Go right ahead,' Michael said, his voice hoarse.

'Please. Demote me. I'm not competent to be your Number One.'

'What aren't you telling us?' the Jade Emperor said.

The Tiger eyed Michael, waiting for his reply.

I killed her, Dad, Michael said to himself. My mother, your wife. I killed the only woman you would give up all the others for. The one you wanted to make your Empress. I found her, and I killed her. The two most important women I've ever known, two fragile humans who were counting on this powerful Shen to protect them, and I murdered them with my stupidity. I killed them.

'Nothing,' Michael said.

'Go home to the Western Palace, and come back when you are willing to share the rest,' the Jade Emperor said.

'Am I demoted?' Michael said.

'No,' the Tiger said. 'I need your administrative skills in the Palace. But in future let your brothers and sisters handle the battle and tactics, you're restricted to paperwork where you won't do any more damage. You led a team of fifteen of my best Horsemen to their deaths, boy, and that's the most *minor* failure in this whole disappointing episode.' He waved Michael away. 'Dismissed.'

Michael rose from the couch, knelt to salute them, and teleported back to his apartment in the Western Palace. He headed straight for the kitchen to find something to drink, the stronger the better.

He didn't know how much later it was. He was lying on the couch, one arm over his eyes and the other holding the coffee mug full of bourbon, when there was a rap on the door. He ignored it, and the rapping turned to knocking. The knocks escalated into bangs, then the door unlocked by itself. He didn't move from the couch when the door opened.

'Immortal or not, that's a breach of privacy.'

'Michael,' Rohan said. 'You've been in here for hours, man. What's going on?'

'Did Dad send you?'

'Yeah.' Rohan came into the living room. 'Good bourbon. Got another cup?'

Michael waved towards the kitchen.

Rohan came back, filled his coffee mug from the bourbon bottle, and sat on the other couch. 'Tell me.'

'No.'

'Something serious happened, man. Share.'

'No.'

Rohan took a swig from his cup, then coughed. 'You were gone for two weeks and won't tell anyone what happened. Did they torture you? Why'd you stay there, when you could just kill yourself and come back? Did they have a way of holding you so you couldn't kill yourself? If they did, you have to tell us about it.' His voice became more intense. 'What the fuck happened to you?'

Michael looked down at his hands holding the bourbon-filled mug and had another drink, feeling the comforting burn down to his belly. 'I thought I'd be able to gather some information while I was there. You know, do something really worthwhile and finally gain some parental approval. Prove that I'm worthy of the position of Number One Son, shit like that. I wasn't up to it, which isn't surprising. If it was you there, with your two-hundred-odd years of training and experience, you'd probably bring home the head of the Demon King himself.'

'Three hundred,' Rohan said into his bourbon. 'But I doubt it. Look at what happened in that nest: we all died straight away and you fought them off.'

'I didn't fight them off. They wanted me for my half-European heritage, and saved me for it.' Michael lay back on the sofa again. 'I'm not good enough.'

Rohan lay back as well. 'Dad thinks you are.'

'Dad thinks I'm the only one stupid enough to put up with being his Number One.'

Rohan chuckled. 'Oh no, he knows for sure that you're the only one stupid enough to put up with it. So tell me about the European Heavens. How do they compare to ours?'

'Oh, Rohan,' Michael said with feeling. 'Let me tell you about one of the most beautiful places I've ever been, and I've been in the Celestial Palace itself.'

Late the next morning, he lay in bed looking at the ceiling for nearly an hour, untying the knots in his aching head. When he couldn't stand the inactivity any more he washed, dressed, grabbed a cup of coffee out of his apartment's little kitchen, and teleported to his office. He fell into the chair behind his desk and opened the email program, then winced when he saw how many messages he had.

There were a pile of notes on his desk as well; several from William.

He contacted his brother telepathically. *William?*

*Oh, hey Mike, welcome back*, William said. *We all missed your rampant assholery around here, Rohan had to fill in and he's not nearly as much of a total bastard.*

*It's good to be back*, Michael said.

*So what happened to you? You were gone for a while, man.*

*I did some stupid shit and failed my mission*, Michael said. He changed the subject. *Hey, did that dragon you were dating get back to you? We still have a hundred tonnes of gold to shift.*

William's voice sounded sheepish. *You know how you warned me about dating dragons?*

*He was cheating on you?*

*He didn't understand why I had an issue with it! He even invited me for a threesome. With a woman!*

*Ooh, tasty. So did you do it? Tell me all!*

*No! For fuck's sake, Michael, what the hell …* William's voice petered out. *Oh, very funny. I can see your face now. Well, too bad, I'm not seeing him any more and there's your financial figures gone. So there.* William shut off communication.

Michael tossed the notes in the waste basket and turned back to the emails. Many of them weren't directly for him; they were panic-stricken Celestials sharing concern about the Dark Lord's foray into the European Heavens and the unpleasant scenario he was discovering – of imminent war with the demons. Fortunately nobody was interested in Michael's own little misadventure.

More than twenty messages were from his father, with the same subject: DEAL. He thought for a moment that the email program had glitched and sent him the same message multiple times, then he opened the first few.

His father had been receiving desperate messages from other Heavenly Bastions, begging him for weapons-grade steel. Every time the Tiger received one, he forwarded it to Michael with the subject changed to DEAL. Michael opened the messages, one at a time, and jotted down how much steel the Celestials needed. Some of the more senior Celestial residents were offering ridiculously generous amounts of Celestial Jade for weapons-quality steel spun with energy to make it a more effective demon killer, something that only the Tiger's children could produce.

He gave up with pencil and paper and opened a

spreadsheet to calculate the amounts. The total of the requests was more than the gold they were holding, so he'd need to find even more metal after he'd had the gold transformed into steel by several of his senior brothers and sisters. He smiled grimly as he added everything up. Even with the discounted sale price he would offer the Celestials because of the war effort, the Western Heavens were about to see a sudden and much needed surge in Celestial income.

He wished he had Clarissa's expertise with the technology as he worked through the figures. He checked the clock on his desk as he did every day; it was nearly time for her to come out for her walk in the garden. He felt a shock down to his feet – it was two weeks and one day since the psychologist had spoken to him. He threw himself out of his chair and bolted to the door. Just as he reached it the phone rang.

He raced back to his desk and answered it.

'Michael, my boy.' Enzio sounded particularly smug. 'Two weeks, where have you been?'

'Look, Enzio,' Michael said with exasperation. 'You know what? Clarissa was twenty times the financial manager that I will ever be, and you treated her like shit because she's a woman. I'm not coming back.'

'I never treated her badly, Michael, that's all in your mind. Young Clarissa was talented, yes, but she didn't have the *aggression*, the *hunger*, that you have. I can offer you a serious pay rise, much better than anything your father can —'

Michael cut him off. 'Enzio, you sexist piece of shit? Go find something long, hard and sharp, and stick it a very long way up your ass, and while you're at it, never call me again.'

Enzio's voice gained a cruel edge. 'You're more man than that, aren't you? Look at you, a slave to a woman, pussy-whipped into submission by a little —'

'Fuck. You.' Michael slammed the phone down and raced out to the garden.

He threw himself to sit on the same bench and tried to calm his breathing as he waited. He didn't pretend to read a book; either she would see him and approach, or … He didn't think about the rest.

The carer wheeled her into the garden and his heart leapt. She saw him; their eyes met. She looked up to speak to her carer and he felt even more excitement. She frowned slightly and spoke again, and the carer replied. The carer wheeled her out of the garden and he slumped with disappointment.

Okay. He had plenty to do. Plenty. Busy. He needed to keep busy. He teleported back to his office and sat behind his desk. He fiddled with the spreadsheet but the numbers didn't mean anything. He shoved the keyboard away, put his arms on the desk and rested his head on them. This was the third time he'd lost her.

He heard a metallic clatter outside his office, and rose to see what was happening. He stopped with shock when he saw that Clarissa was attempting to wheel herself into the building, her clawed hands having difficulty gaining traction on the wheels as she tried to push herself through the doorway. She hadn't seen him; she was concentrating on coming through the door, hitting the frame with a metallic rattle with each attempt.

'Um …' he said.

She glanced up and saw him, and her expression went stern. 'Why are you just standing there? Help me!'

'Can I give you a push?'

'Of course you can,' she said, releasing the wheels to wave one hand furiously at him. The wheelchair rocketed backwards and he raced to stop it, then took the handles and pushed it into his office.

'Stop here,' she said at his desk. 'I need to talk to you.'

He parked her at his desk then stood in front of her. He studied her gaunt lines and fragile skin, and loved her even more. Her soft fragrance filled the air and he cursed his half-tiger senses. It would kill him to say goodbye.

'She argued with me when I asked her to take me to you, she said you're the reason I'm like this.'

'She's right,' he said.

Clarissa held her hand out and he hesitated. She pushed it at him, and he took it.

Everything went completely still for a moment as he stood dazed and dazzled by her touch.

She leaned her weight on his hand and he held her as she pulled herself up to stand on her own. Her smile widened as she quivered with the effort of standing, grasping his hand with all her might.

She lost her balance and he grabbed her other hand before she could topple. She lowered herself to sit in the chair, still holding both his hands, and he knelt on one knee in front of her.

'I did it,' she said, her voice full of triumph.

'You did,' he said.

She pulled at his hands and he moved closer. She closed her eyes and remained unmoving for a moment. She released his hand, slipped it behind his head, and pulled him in so quickly that he was kissing her before he knew what was happened. He stiffened with shock, then fell into the chasm of joy that was the feeling of being with her again. He put his arms around her and held her as she massaged the back of his head and ran her fingers through his hair. Her hand slipped onto his cheek and she pulled back to see him, her eyes full of doubt.

'I probably can't have children,' she said.

'I don't care,' he said.

'You're Immortal and I'm just a weak and mortal human.'

'I don't care.'

'I'll be permanently disabled, I'll never be as strong as I was —'

'Clarissa, my love.' He cut her off. 'I *don't care*. All I care about is you, and I want to be with you. Always.'

'Are you really sure, Michael?'

'I've never been more sure of anything. I want to be with you for the rest of your life. Do you still want to be with me?'

She took a deep breath and her eyes sparkled with tears. 'Always.'

He kissed her again and tasted her tears, and something rang like a great bell deep inside him. This was the real Clarissa. This was her. There was no doubt.

She rested her forehead on his. 'Always.' She pulled back to smile into his eyes. 'Hey.'

'Hmm?'

'I've really missed flying. Take me out, please?'

'What, right now?'

She nodded.

He picked her up out of the chair like a child and carried her out of his office. She put her arms around his neck and smiled, the tears running down her face.

'Hold on tight!' he shouted, and shot straight into the air.

She shrieked with delight, and the skies of the Heavens rang with her peals of laughter.

Extract From

KYLIE CHAN'S DARK HEAVENS
BOOK ONE
WHITE TIGER

'Mother, Leo,' Simone whispered.
'Oh my God,' Leo said under his breath.
I readied myself and hefted my sword. 'I'm right behind you.'
'Stay there. Don't get in the way. If I go down …' He hesitated. 'Don't let it have you, Emma. It won't hurt her, she'll be okay. But whatever you do, don't let it take you.'
'I understand.'
The demon appeared in the doorway.
Its back end was a slimy snake that oozed toxin over its black scales. The front end looked like the top half of a man with the skin taken off. It had to lower itself onto its coils to fit through the door; it was enormous.
It came halfway into the room and raised its body on the coils. Its skinless head nearly touched the ceiling.
'You are the Black Lion? Disciple of the Dark Lord?'
'I am just an ordinary man.'
The demon smiled and its red eyes flashed. 'I like your skin. I think I will take it.'
Leo readied himself. 'Come and get it.'

*Find more about Kylie's books at her website:
www.kyliechan.com*